Stellar Harmony

Morgan Sterling

Morgan Sterling

Contents

1. Chapter 1   1

2. Chapter 2   13

3. Chapter 3   23

4. Chapter 4   34

5. Chapter 5   57

6. Chapter 6   75

7. Chapter 7   94

8. Chapter 8   103

9. Chapter 9   122

10. Chapter 10   131

11. Chapter 11   143

12. Chapter 12   156

13. Chapter 13   166

14. Chapter 14   186

15. Chapter 15 — 193

16. Epilogue — 209

Also by Morgan Sterling — 216

Let's Keep In Touch — 217

About the author — 219

17. Soft Reset preview — 220

Feedback? — 238

Chapter 1

Langston

I sat back in the curved velvet chair, my eyebrows set in a deep furrow. I didn't want to be here—a lounge on Friday night jam-packed with rapping wannabes and overly emotional spoken word artists.

The lounge buzzed with anticipation and creativity, the air thick with the scents of perfume and cologne mingling with the smoky haze of dimmed lights. Aspiring artists, poets, and musicians filled the space, their voices blending into a cacophony of laughter and impassioned conversation. The energy was apparent even to me, each person eager to take their turn at the microphone and share their latest masterpiece.

Amidst the vibrant chaos, I sat in a curved velvet chair, feeling like an anomaly in my own world. I scanned the room, taking in the eclectic mix of people who had come together for this open mic night.

Various styles and attitudes on display, from the confident swagger of rappers exchanging verses to the vulnerability of spoken word artists pouring their souls out through carefully crafted lines.

I swirled the brown liquor in my short glass, watching the large square ice cube swirl around. It reminded me of a centrifuge.

Even with the pulsating energy around me, I felt detached. The world of academia and astrophysics were a totally different universe than I was in tonight.

In the corner of my eye Malcolm, my childhood best friend, laughed and joked with other patrons. Malcolm had talked me into coming tonight, insisting that it would do me some good to "loosen up" and experience the artistic side of our hometown.

I should've stayed home and graded papers, I mused internally, taking a sip of my drink as I continued to observe the room. A long to-do list rattled through my head, and all I was thinking of was the unfinished stack of research papers waiting for my attention back at the apartment.

"Come on, man, don't be such a killjoy," Malcolm said, standing over me suddenly, pulling my thoughts back to the room. "This place is full of talent and inspiration. Who knows? Maybe you'll find a muse among these poets and singers."

I allowed myself a small smile at the thought, shaking my head. "Yeah, perhaps. But I think I'll stick to observing from a safe distance. Plus, I got stuff to do. If you'd hurry up and get up there and read your stuff instead of posing around here chasing tail-"

Malcolm smacked his teeth.

"Nigga, please. It's early. Gotta wait till the house gets packed a bit. Why you in a rush to get back across town and do nothing?"

"Nothing? I wouldn't call my work 'nothing,' Malcolm," I replied defensively, my fingers tapping the side of the glass in agitation. "I have a lot on my plate, you know."

"First black professor of Astrophysics in UC--check. Summa Cum Laude; Ivy League alumnus--check. Alien-hunting grant proposals—checkmark hell. But for now, relax, Langston. Everything will still be there when we leave," Malcolm reassured, placing a hand on my shoulder. "But right now, we're here. So let's enjoy it and live in the moment a little."

I sighed, knowing that Malcolm was right. I needed to find a way to balance life between the academic world I'd built for myself and the one I left behind in the old neighborhood. I had a choice of universities when I took a position. I'd selected the one that brought me back to my hometown--Shytown.

And while it was always there, following me even when I was at a university overseas, the sense of being an imposter was worse here. I'd grown up in the hood miles from the place where all my credentials hung. My parents had died, so I had no reason to go back to the old neighborhood. But honestly, I wanted to go more often, even if it was for dinner or to play ball. I really only went whenever I was visiting Malcolm.

I never felt quite whole, no matter where I was, but I just didn't know how to merge the two. The constant push and pull of my two worlds left me an outsider in both.

"Alright, fine," I relented, forcing a more genuine smile. "I'll try to loosen up a bit and enjoy the night."

"Good man!" Malcolm exclaimed with a grin, clapping me on the back. "Trust me, you won't regret it. Now, let's get ready for some incredible performances."

Malcolm slid into a matching purple seat. We were facing out, allowing us to look out into the room of milling bodies. I looked over at him, realizing we made an odd pair. Malcolm was tall and wiry, baby-faced, with long locs in an unruly ponytail. His white teeth stood out against his mocha-smooth skin. And when he flashed a smile at a woman, usually followed by some irresistible line full of bullshit, he never left places like this alone.

On the other hand, I was what Malcolm called "short tall"... taller than most guys, but never the tallest guy in the room. And where Malcolm's muscles were hidden in a wiry frame, I was wide-shouldered, broad-chested, and strong. My light skin was set off by the deep brown hair I kept in a low fade. My mustache tapered around my mouth, joining the shadow of a beard. My mouth was currently set in a frown, and I had no smooth words for anybody—especially for women spilling half their titties out a dress. I was a man, and I loved a beautiful body, but it took more than that to catch my eye in a world where you could buy bodies made to order.

Malcolm looked back at me, probably registering that I had mentally exited the room again.

"Earth to Dr. Wilkerson. It's the weekend. We clear across town, away from that bougie school. You need to take a break. Besides," Malcolm leaned forward and gestured to the crowd. "You ain't got no good ass like this walking around that vanilla campus."

I rolled my eyes. Malcolm wasn't saying the campus was vanilla because it was mostly Caucasian, which it was. He meant vanilla as in boring—which it absolutely was. It wasn't the kind of school with Frat Parties as much as it was the kind that had Nobel Prize Laureate welcoming dinners.

"Malcolm, you know as well as I do that I've got a ton of work to catch up on. The grant committee is breathing down my neck, and I can't afford to waste any time," I sighed, swirling the liquor in my glass, watching the amber liquid spin.

"Man, you're always working," Malcolm shook his head, his locs swaying with the movement. "What happened to the Langston who used to sneak out to parties over your summer break back in the day? You remember those nights, right?"

I couldn't help but crack a smile at the memory. "Yeah, I remember. But we were kids back then, Malcolm. Things are different now. I've got responsibilities."

"Responsibilities, schmonsibilities," Malcolm waved me off, taking a sip of his drink. "You're still young, Langston. You deserve to have some fun every once in a while. Besides, your brain can use a break from all that astrophysics mumbo-jumbo."

"Maybe you're right," I admitted reluctantly, glancing around the lively lounge filled with the energy of aspiring artists. I'd been stuck on a specific problem and Dr. Davis, my mentor, had said that taking a break from it and exposing myself to different ideas and thoughts would probably help. If this nightclub was anything, it was different than the quiet halls of academia I'd grown accustomed to. But it was something undeniably appealing about it – something that tugged at a part of me I'd long since buried beneath equations and research papers.

"Of course, I'm right," Malcolm grinned. "Now, let's enjoy this night, and who knows? Inspiration for your next big discovery may be right here in this room."

With a resigned chuckle, I raised my glass in a toast. "Alright, Malcolm. Let's see what this night has in store for us."

As we continued to chat, I couldn't help but become mesmerized by the light glinting off the brown liquor in the short glass. The dim lighting of the lounge reflected off of its amber color, casting a warm, inviting glow that urged me to let go of my worries just for one night.

My mind wandered back to the grant committee which had been relentlessly pressuring me to produce groundbreaking results from my research. Their expectations weighed heavily on my shoulders. Plus, if I significantly contributed to the field of astrophysics, I might finally feel like I belonged somewhere.

"Langston," Malcolm's voice pulled me out of my thoughts. "You're doing it again, man. You're here, but your mind is somewhere else. I'm telling you, you need to loosen up and live a little."

"Sorry, Malcolm," shaking my head as if trying to physically dislodge the burdens that weighed on me. "You're right. I'll try to be more present."

Malcolm clapped me on the shoulder once while he swiveled his head to follow a petite, full-figured woman who sauntered by. She looked over her shoulder at Malcolm , who unabashedly proclaimed, "Damn!"

Malcolm caught the woman's attention, stood, and began to approach her while performing an impromptu rap about how beautiful she was. She giggled and gave Malcolm her number. I rolled my eyes but couldn't help but marvel at my friend's ability to captivate another human with such ease... especially when he was on that bullshit.

Malcolm grinned as he returned to his seat, flipping the number the woman gave him between his fingertips. I had to laugh. "That's what I'm talking about! You don't have to choose between being a professor and being true to your roots. You can do both! Go shoot your shot at one of these fine women."

"Man, black chicks like this don't want me. And I ain't got enough energy to fake interest in whatever they are talking about just to hit it."

Malcolm sighed and nodded. Years ago he'd witnessed my awkward efforts to talk to the girls from around the way. Growing up, they'd girls always said I was too square, weird, or out there. Malcolm had been there to see all of my early crushes and every rejection. Blerds, aka Black Nerds, didn't become sexy until we were both grown, and Donald Glover had shown the world that Nerd Niggas be hot too. But by then, it was too late. My brain had long since pulled me out of the hood to the Ivy Leagues on scholarship, then out of the country to study my passion, Astrophysics. By the time I'd returned home for good a few months ago to take up the position at the university, I was different--at least when it came to women. I wasn't scrawny and hunched over textbooks. I wasn't wearing second-hand clothes because that was all my parents were able to afford.

My years in the gym were easy to see under my clothes. When I didn't quite fit in at whatever college I was at, I always felt at home working out. And now I wore a lot of urban styles, with nods to my passion for the stars. Sometimes, it was a sparkling diamond piece on my wrist, like the one I sported tonight; it reminded me of the stars that fascinated me during the day.

Chicks I ran into at places like this tried to connect if they got through the rough, usually frowning, exterior. I was as stubborn as I was brilliant and had long since made up my mind that African American women were beautiful to look at but would never, ever be interested in me for a relationship. Even though Malcolm had insisted that now, it was a case of me not giving them a shot, I wasn't so sure.

"Ladies and Gentlemen, welcome." A voice from the stage caught my attention. A tall woman with thin locs in an updo stood before a retro-style microphone. She wore bold red lipstick, loose purple and gold harem pants, and a matching shirt.

Aurora

This was not the way I wanted to spend my first Friday night in town. I'd specifically come to Chicago, of all of my choices of escape, because it was currently cold, gray, and icky—like my soul. That, and of course, my favorite Aunt lives here. All I wanted to do was stay under the covers and sleep. And Aunt Cecily had promised on the phone I'd be able to unplug.

But here I am, on a cold Friday night, in Aunt Cecily's weekly spot for Open Mic. She stood in the spotlight, looking regal in her purple, welcoming all the faces.

While at first, it looked like there wouldn't be too many people, the place had filled up in a short period of time. I'm so happy that Aunt Cecily sat at a reserved table in a roped-off area.

"... And some guests that are amazingly talented. I hope some of them get up here and share with us..."

I zoned back in just in time to hear a portion of the welcome speech I was sure was directed at me.

Not happening. There was no way I'm getting up there sharing my soul—especially after what had just happened the weeks prior. The sting of betrayal was too recent.

Still, Aunt Cecily was amazing and gracious and looked out for me. So I plastered a smile on my face as she returned to the table. At least I can pretend like my mind wasn't already made up.

"Baby girl, I'm so happy you agreed to come tonight." Aunt Cecily patted me on the hand. "This is exactly what the doctor ordered to cleanse your soul."

I smiled faintly and watched as a large, curvy woman with a puffed-out 'fro took the stage. She wore a leopard print top, a suede red mini skirt, a black leather cincher belt, and knee-high boots. She looked out to the crowd, and her ruby red lips parted to reveal a sharp tongue—half street preacher, half angel.

Have you ever felt like looking at the sun
And saying Fuck This Shit, not today?
Because yesterday you were promised a miracle
The day before that, you were promised a change
And the day before that, you were promised opportunity
But everyday was the same?
The same job treating you like Job—
Pushing down on your good soul?
The same lying ass nigga telling the same lies—
Cause he thinks you fell for them before?
The same sister, cousin, uncle treating you like a bank—
And you're just sitting on the bank trying to decide whether to jump in and drown,
Or jump in and swim?

A few mutters of understanding came from the crowd. I found myself nodding too.

Guess what?
You don't owe nobody nothing
Not even the sun.

Let your soul be on the run, cause today-?
Shit, today you're not the one.

A few people cackled and laughed, and the crowd began to clap.

"Yeah, Gina, that's how we start this thing!"

I looked up to see an extremely tall, dark chocolate man standing, one hand cupped to his mouth while the other gestured wildly.

If I had been paying attention, I would have seen the exciting performer give a wink to the man as she vacated the stage.

But I wasn't looking at the woman or the yelling man. I was too busy looking at the hulking man who was seated beside the man. He swirled bourbon in his glass like he wished it were gasoline. He didn't even look like he was in the same room.

While everyone clapped, he frowned.

"What the hell is his problem?" I muttered to myself, wondering what kind of Grinch would bring bad vibes to an open mic night. God, I didn't want to be here either, but at least I could smile and clap for the brave folks who got up there to bear their souls.

"Hmm?" Cecily said, following my gaze toward the two men. "Oh, that's just Malcolm. He's always that loud and verbose. Here every week, always something new from him. Wait until it's his turn." Her eyes twinkled.

Before I was able to ask any questions, the sound of two men taking the stage to a series of clucking noises from the audience tore away the attention of my aunt, who herself had immediately joined in.

This place is crazy. But I had to admit, the two men who did a tag team cipher about the effects of poverty on their neighborhood were hypnotic. When they finished, everyone was clucking again.

I cast an inquisitive look to my aunt, who laughed. "The larger one is named Chester. Like Chester's Chicken. The little one is named Colin. Like Colonel Colin Powell. Colonel. KFC. Chicken-?"

I raised an eyebrow. "So y'all cluck?"

My aunt laughed as she headed back to the stage.

When the spotlight bathed her in light and attention, she addressed the relaxed, muttering crowd.

"Alright now. Always bringing the consciousness, those brothers. Thank you." She turned and gave applause to the two who had returned to the bar.

"Now, speaking of conscience, let's welcome up X."

I watched the tall, wiry man I'd seen earlier bound up the stairs, stopping long enough to grab what looked like a djembe.

It wasn't the performance that I expected. Normally, open mic was people vocalizing in some way. But Malcolm had only shot a wide smile to the crowd before he began to let his hands say everything.

The musician in me had to admit it was beautiful. I was so focused that I almost didn't hear my aunt say Malcolm's performances were always different. Sometimes, he spoke; other times, he played instruments, like he'd chosen to do this night.

With one last beat, he flipped his head back, removing a loose loc that had strayed into his face. His big smile cued the applause. Even I had to give it to him—he was a performance artist.

My eyes followed him back to his seat, where the once gloomy man with him was turned into a beautiful beam of joy. I noticed he had a small nose ring, portions of one eyebrow razor bladed off, and a beautiful smile. And beautiful eyes. He was far away, but everything I could see from where I was sitting was beautiful.

I stared so hard that I didn't realize what my aunt had said when a spotlight panned onto me. The man I was looking at was now looking at me, head cocked to the side, looking me up and down. My body flushed hot and I crossed my arms under my breasts suddenly hyper-aware of my nipples against thin velvet. When I looked around I realized everyone was looking at me.

"Please?" Aunt Cecily said in a sweet, whiny voice. "One quick one, Aurora? Please?"

I huffed, then put on a fake smile as I stood and moved towards the stage.

That's why I should have stayed my ass home, was all I thought as I took the microphone from my aunt, who quickly vacated the stage.

Chapter 2

Aurora

The dimly lit room held a sense of anticipation, the audience's chatter softening as I stepped onto the stage. Shadows slithered along the patina-stained walls, and the scent of spiced candles intermingled with the tang of alcohol and perfume. My heart beat in time to the rhythm to my heeled pumps, each step bringing me closer to the microphone that beckoned me like a lover.

I felt the room's gaze upon me as I stood beneath the warm glow of the spotlight. The murmurs of an unfamiliar crowd died down, their faces masked by a concoction of curiosity, anticipation, and a trace of hope. Aunt Cecily told everyone I was her niece, so I knew they were expecting great things. It was a bonus and burden of being from a well-known artistic family--expectations.

I closed my eyes briefly, took a deep breath, and let the room's energy wash over me.

"Good evening," I whispered into the microphone. I heard the flexs of seductive smokiness in my voice. It was automatic to put on my stage voice. I didn't even have to think about it.

An immediate silence fell over the crowd, punctuated by sporadic whistles from enthusiastic onlookers. I sensed the room on edge, hanging onto every syllable I uttered. "Tonight, I want to unveil an acapella version—a sincere take—on a song that has always been dear to me."

My fingers clutched onto the microphone stand, subtly betraying my jittery nerves to anyone who looked close enough. I embarked on a musical journey from the first note that flowed through my lips. The music slipped its reins. A honeyed spell fell over—enchanting both me and my listeners. The melodious tune cascaded from my lips like molten honey dripping down bare skin, absorbed in every note.

Each note carried with it a piece of me—my dreams, fears, desires, and vulnerabilities. I was giving a piece of myself to each of these strangers... and it felt good.

In that moment, I was more than a singer; I was a conduit for the emotions that tied us all together, a bridge between the world of art and the realities of life.

Unthinking, my hips found their primal cadence, flesh answering sultry vocals with ancestral memory. It was as if I sung this song in all my previous lives. It's sensual nature seemed to permeate the air around me, leaving a tangible sense of being connected to something bigger than I was.

As I reached a crescendo, an energy coursed through my veins, like an electric wildfire racing beneath collarbone, down my spine, and between my legs. Music allowed me to experience the full spectrum of emotions, and this song lit my soul on goddamn fire. My eyes roved over the audience, craving a connection, a lifeline to anchor me in this otherworldly moment. Someone to share this with.

Then I saw him.

Our gazes locked, and fuck if time itself didn't grind to a halt. An invisible force pulled me towards him, his dark gaze burning hotter than any stage spotlight. I didn't dare tear myself away - hell, I didn't want to.

My song became tongue against his ear, practically begging him to comprehend just how naked I felt before him in that moment. It was as if we were the only two beings in existence, bound together by the pure sexual current that popped and sparked between us like live wires.

If he felt even half of what I did... God help us both.

Langston

My heart hammered in my chest as I watched Aurora perform. I didn't really know much about the arts beyond my best friend, Malcolm. I didn't connect with most artists. They were hearts and emotions. I was data and facts.

But something about this woman captivated me in a way I'd never experienced.

I leaned forward until my chair creaked, eyes devouring her every move as she crooned. Heat overtook me, and I found my lips dry. I darted my tongue out to moisten them and immediately wondered what she'd taste like.

What the hell is wrong with me? As a man of cold logic, this unexpected magnetic lust made no damn sense. It was as if some primal force awakened—one refusing to be ignored.

As her song climaxed, one thing was crystal clear: I had to get this woman alone after her tantalizing performance. It seemed like a crazy idea, but I couldn't ignore that our connection was more than a coincidence or fluke.

The final note of her song hung in the air, echoing through my mind. I had butterflies at the idea of approaching her when she got off the stage. Navigating the academic world was easy, but when it came to social interactions - especially with someone who captivated me so entirely - my confidence faltered. My heart raced and my palms grew slick as I rummaged my mind for the perfect words to say.

Malcolm nudged me. "Man, she was definitely singing to you," he said with a smirk on his face. "You better go talk to her before someone else does."

"Maybe I should," I murmured, still not quite believing the intensity of the connection I had with this woman I hadn't even spoken to yet. I observed as Aurora gracefully glid through the crowd, her curly 'fro bouncing with each step and her body radiating otherworldly energy. The audience members praised her, and she acknowledged it with polite nods.

The men around her seemed drawn to her like moths to a flame, attempting to catch her attention with flirty gestures and compliments.

My eyes took in how her dress clung to every curve, accentuating her alluring figure with every step she took. The cloth moved taunt over her curves, the dip of her waist, and the flawlessly round bottom.

I took a deep, shaky breath, trying to silence the voice of doubt that consumed me. I slowly rose from my seat and cautiously made my way across the room, heart racing with anticipation and fear. *Was she about to reject me? Am I about to get embarrassed? She clearly hadn't been interested in any of the other guys that had approached her. Hell, did she even like guys?* I couldn't stop my mind from racing as I approached her.

I hesitated for a moment, struggling to find the right words. Finally, I decided to jump in headfirst.

"Your performance was... incredible," I said, my voice low and slightly rough, betraying my nervousness.

She turned around to face me, her expression initially one of surprise but then quickly melting into a warm smile. Her eyes sparkled with curiosity and seemed to search my own for something deeper, as if she was trying to unravel a mystery. "Thank you," her voice was sincere and held a hint of gratitude.

I was surprised that the words came after that, and speaking to her was easy. As we sipped on our glasses of confidence, the clinking of ice cube against my glass was a subtle background melody adding to the atmosphere of our conversation. My own voice sounded foreign to me as I spoke to Aurora, my words smooth and easy as if I had rehearsed them many times before.

She leaned in to listen to me over the performers' sounds and the lounge's conversations. And as if automatically, I leaned in, too. And the smell that wafered off her was amazing. *What was it? Coconut?*

My fingertips tingled with electricity as I traced patterns on the smooth surface of the glass of whiskey. I saw a hint of ink on her shoulder. *What would it be like to trace the outline of that tattoo? I wonder what it is?*

"Wait, so you're *Doctor* Wilkerson? An astrophysicist?" she purred, her eyes sparkling with admiration. I felt a surge of pride at her genuine interest but tried not to show it. I shrugged, trying to play down my accomplishments.

"Guilty as charged," I responded with a half-smile. "I guess you could say I'm more at home among the stars than here on Earth."

"Maybe you can show me the stars sometime?" Aurora suggested with a playful grin. "I've always been fascinated by the mysteries of the universe."

Aurora

I found myself anchored to the bar. Tonight's performance reverberated inside me- a unique blend of euphoria and exhaustion that only comes from baring your soul on stage. My music style, raw and unfiltered, seemed to stir an unseen connection between me and the audience.

"One Pinot Noir, please," I requested languidly to the bartender, lost in a flood of introspective thought. I thought of the fleeting moment when my gaze met that man in the crowd. His presence scorched through her defenses – sudden oxygen feeding banked embers.

I was so deep in thought I didn't notice another man attempting to make his intentions known through an all-too-confident stride. But tonight wasn't about entertaining strangers' attention.

"I hate to disappoint you," my voice cut through the air before he could utter his rehearsed pick-up line, "but I'm good."

The man's face fell, but he nodded and walked away, leaving me to my thoughts. I took a sip of the wine that had been handed to me, savoring its rich flavor while I tried to focus on the warmth it brought rather than the lingering gazes from other men in the bar.

"Your performance was... incredible," rumbled a deep, gravelly voice from behind jolting me out of my solitude. The intrusion wasn't what rattled me, but the way his cutting words invaded my sanctuary.

"Excuse me?" I snapped, turning to face the source of the voice. But when I saw it was *him*, his eyes ablaze with raw admiration, the fire of irritation began to smolder into something else.

The man's husky voice rolled through me like thunder cracking dry brush. A sensation, something I hadn't experienced in eons, washed over me. My pulse pounded out a wild rhythm, my skin prickled with anticipation - an instinctive response to his presence. I fought against the gravitational tug of his voice; every syllable dragged me forward until barstool vinyl creaked under my shifting weight. Heat pooled low as my pulse drummed triple-time – traitorous body spotlighting everything his grin promised.

My eyes traced the contours of his muscled physique, fingers twitching with phantom memory of how such hardness melted under touch.

"Thank you," I said, my voice wavering from the intensity of the emotions coursing through me. "I'm glad you enjoyed it."

He nodded, his eyes never leaving mine. "You have a gift. The way you connect with your audience... it's special."

As we continued to talk, the world around us seemed to fade away, replaced by the intense connection that was forming between us. Despite our different backgrounds and interests, we were drawn to one another – two souls seeking solace in each other's company.

"Your name is perfect because your performance reminded me of a supernova," Langston said with a bit of humor in his voice. "Bright, explosive, and unforgettable."

I laughed, at ease with his lighthearted compliment. "Well, I've never been compared to a celestial event before! You must be quite the stargazer."

"Actually, yes," he admitted, smiling. "I've always found comfort in looking up at the night sky."

"Me too. Something about the vastness makes my problems seem small and insignificant."

"Exactly," Langston said, leaning closer. "It's like the universe is telling us that we're all connected in some way. Even when we're alone, we're all part of something much bigger."

As time passed, our conversation flowed effortlessly, ranging from discussions about music and space to playful banter about everything under the sun. We teased each other, danced around our attraction, and occasionally let our eyes linger just a little too long, hinting at the undeniable chemistry.

"Basslines live in your hips first," I murmured, letting my voice dip to a sinful whisper. "The vibrations find marrow before ears."

"Is that right?" Langston asked, one eyebrow arching in a suggestive manner. His gaze wandered over my body appreciatively. "I can't say I've ever felt that... physical connection to music, but the way you describe it... I'm fucking intrigued."

"Maybe someday I'll give you a personal demonstration," I proposed seductively.

"Is that a promise or a threat?" he shot back, matching my flirtatious banter. He was now bolder with his looks, his eyes full of admiration and anticipation.

"You'll just have to stick around long enough to find out," I teased. My laughter danced through the charged atmosphere, blending with his deep, throaty chuckle.

"So, what do you do for a living?" I asked. I leaned in, listening to the deep bass in his voice. It was giving raw sex.

"I'm an astrophysicist," he revealed. "I teach at the local university."

"Professor Langston-?"

"Dr. Wilkerson, actually."

"Wait, so you're *Doctor* Wilkerson? An astrophysicist?" I asked incredulously, impressed by the revelation. Langston merely shrugged.

"Guilty as charged," he responded with a half-smile. "I guess you could say I'm more at home among the stars than here on Earth."

"Maybe you can show me the stars sometime?" I suggested with a playful grin. "I've always been fascinated by the mysteries of the universe."

His eyes lingered on me, but he didn't respond.

"Still," I insisted, "it takes a special kind of dedication and intelligence to reach that level. Don't sell yourself short. So you get in front of people like me? Your students."

Langston smiled. "I guess. Others sometimes, too. In fact, I'm giving a star talk that is open to the community next week. We'll be using the observatory telescope. You should come. Maybe we'll see a Supernova. Probably not as pretty as you, but still."

I couldn't help but smile, my eyes lingering on his lips as he ran a warm pink tongue along the bottom one.

"That would be nice."

He smiled, took out a pen, and wrote his number on a cocktail napkin, and slid it to me.

"Unfortunately, I have to get going. My friend has work early tomorrow, and he can't stay out too late." He looked over toward the door where his tall friend was chatting it up with a girl while he was putting on his coat. He did look like he was ready to leave.

I tried to hide my disappointment, nodding understandingly. "Of course, I get it. I wouldn't want to keep anyone from their responsibilities."

"Believe me, I wish I was able to stay here all night and talk to you," Langston said, sincerity shining in his eyes. "But maybe we can continue this another time?"

I hesitated for a moment before allowing a hopeful smile. "I'd like that, Langston."

"Great," he replied, his smile wide and genuine. Standing up to leave, he took one last look at me as if trying to memorize my features.

"Goodnight, Aurora," he said low, reluctance evident in his voice.

"Goodnight, Langston," I replied, watching him walk out into the night's cold air, taking with him the brief feeling of warmth he'd give me.

Chapter 3

Langston

As I stare out my office window, the images of Aurora's expressive eyes and her wild mane of hair dance behind my eyelids like a haunting melody. I can almost hear her voice, deep and throaty, as it lets out notes. It makes the hairs on the back of my neck stand up. And honestly, it stirs a primal response lower down.

I'm supposed to be practicing my Star Tours Talk, part of a series I do for the community. Really, only students and donors show up, but the general public is invited. *I wonder if she'll show up.* My fascination with Aurora has grown exponentially since our first encounter, drawn to her creative gravity and emotional transparency. Yet, with each step closer to her, my insecurities pulled me back.

I sigh, acutely aware that being an astrophysics professor is a universe away from Aurora's emotionally charged rhythm and blues performances. Feelings of inadequacy creep in as I wonder if she views me as just another nerd who can't appreciate the depths of her spirit.

"Hey, Professor Wilkerson," a voice calls out, breaking me from my daydream.

"Jamal, what can I do for you?" I ask, turning toward the young student who reminds me so much of my younger self. He was younger than other students in my program because, like me, he had skipped several grades and completed college courses before graduating high school. And like me, he didn't look the way people normally assumed a kid with that academic trajectory should look. Today, he had on a pair of old-school flip-up glasses that doubled as shades. I couldn't help but smile thinking about the day he'd come to my office to tell *me* that *he'd* discovered a show called A Different World that I would like. I told him he had discovered the show like Columbus had discovered America. The boy hadn't been without the trademark glasses since.

Today, he also wore gym shorts and a T-shirt from his high school in the old neighborhood. His parents were still alive, and he lived there and loved showing off his connection to the old stomping ground.

I wonder if, like me, his connection would weaken once he finished the program here and went off to another institution in another part of the world like I had.

"I hope I'm not interrupting you. I wanted to inquire about today's Star Tours Lecture– we're covering The Eagle Nebula, correct?"

"That's right," I confirm, energized at the mention of my heavenly obsession. "Are you planning on attending?"

"Absolutely! I can't wait." Jamal's pen taps staccato rhythms against his notebook.

"Great, see you there," I nod. As Jamal leaves, I allow myself one more lingering thought of Aurora before immersing myself in the preparations for my talk. I can't deny it, that girl is sexy as hell. But sitting at that bar that night was probably the closest I'd ever come to her.

When I enter the lecture hall, no wild mane catches my eye between the orderly rows. She isn't coming. Ridiculous--we just met.

Still, I find myself swallowing my disappointment. I can't shake the thought she is sand in an hourglass I can't flip.

When I approached the podium, I saw Jamal sitting front and center, practically bouncing excitedly. At least I still have the stars – and students like Jamal, who share my passion for discovery.

"Good evening, everyone. I'm Langston Wilkerson, a professor of astrophysics here at the University of Chicago. Tonight, we'll discuss one of our galaxy's most fascinating star-forming regions: The Eagle Nebula."

The feelings of inadequacy seem to melt off me. I strut my melanated frame across the stage. "Now, the Eagle Nebula, also named Messier 16, is a vast region located about 7,000 light-years away from Earth," I begin, my voice brimming with excitement. "It's a stellar nursery where new stars are being born as we speak."

I click the control in my hand, and a screen that takes up the entire stage wall flickers to life with a picture of a stunning collage of radiant colors. It's a photo of colossal pillars of interstellar dust and gas, washed in hues that made hydrogen alpha emissions look beautiful--celestial blues and radiant pinks. The audience gasps as they take in the picture. Even I have to stop and stare, though I've seen it hundreds of times.

Beautiful.

"The beauty of the Eagle Nebula lies in its stunning pillars of gas and dust," I continue, gesturing toward a captivating image of towering structures illuminated by nearby stars. "These pillars are often called the 'Pillars of Creation,' and for good reason."

As I begin describing the nebula's pillars of gas and dust, I think of Aurora. Like those cosmic clouds, she is a mystery waiting to be unraveled. My gaze drifts to the empty seat where I imagine her sitting.

I shake off the fantasy, focusing on the audience before me.

"Within these pillars, new stars are being created due to the immense gravity of the surrounding dust and gas," I explain, my voice filled with passion. "Over time, this material collapses, forming dense cores that will eventually ignite and become new stars."

A woman near the front raises her hand. "Professor Wilkerson, how long does it take for a star to form within the Eagle Nebula?"

"Ah, excellent question," I reply, a smile spreading across my face. "The process can take millions of years, but it's worth noting that, in cosmic terms, that's just the blink of an eye."

I continue my talk, weaving together complex astrophysics concepts with relatable analogies, making the subject accessible even to those without a background in science. The audience is captivated, their eyes glued to me as I unravel the mysteries of the universe before them.

"Professor Wilkerson," another audience member chimes in, "it's fascinating to think about the unimaginable scale of these processes. How do you cope with the vastness when studying the cosmos?"

"Indeed, it can be overwhelming at times," I admit, pausing shortly. "But I find comfort in knowing that we're all part of this grand cosmic story, connected through the very elements that make up our bodies – elements that were forged in the hearts of stars."

As I speak, I can't help but steal another glance at the seat where I had hoped to see Aurora. And there she is, slipping into the room as quietly as possible, her cheeks flushed with embarrassment. A wave of relief washes over me.

"...and so, by understanding the formation of stars within the Eagle Nebula, we gain insight into our own origins and the intricate tapestry of the universe," I say, my eyes locked with Aurora's as if photons from ancient stars connect us both to this moment and eternity.

Aurora

My heart hammered in my chest as I entered the lecture hall late. I tried unsuccessfully not to draw attention to myself, gathering the curious gazes of others as I hurried to find an empty seat. The embarrassment burned in my cheeks, but I took solace in the fact that I had made it – even if I was late.

While I listened, I took in his physical appearance. Today, he looked different – sexier even. Dressed in a sharp, custom-fitted charcoal-gray suit, he rocked a crisp, white shirt, leaving the top buttons open for a laid-back touch. I could see his well-defined collarbone hinting at the strong chest beneath his shirt. And his shoes? Shell-toe Adidas with gray stripes and red laces. I found myself grinning from ear to ear as I took him in.

Maybe I would have stayed my ass in college if my professors looked like this.

It was at this moment that something electric passed between us. Even from my seat, I sensed our shared connection beyond physical attraction. It was as if our souls recognized each other.

As Langston delved deeper into his seductive spiel about the cosmos, my body began to respond instinctively, the fabric of my clothes tight against my awakening desire.

"...and as these stars come alive and morph through time, they create the very foundation of life," he whispered, his voice deep as the ocean's abyss, stirring a resonant echo within the deepest corners of my being. "You could say we're all just stardust, tangled in a cosmic dance spanning light years apart."

He looked right at me, and I swear every pulse between my thighs synchronized with his words.

At that moment, rational thought dissolved into pure sensation. How could I be so consumed with lust for a man speaking about stars? But as I gazed at Langston and absorbed the intensity of his words, I realized there was no denying the fiery longing boiling within me. It was raw and real, overwhelming me with each racing heartbeat.

A few hours later, Langston and I found ourselves at a small, intimate restaurant, the dim lighting casting a soft glow on our faces. The atmosphere was warm and inviting, with a low hum of chatter from other diners creating a comforting sense of anonymity.

"Langston," I said, taking a sip of my wine. "I am curious - how did you get into astrophysics?"

He looked thoughtful for a moment then shrugged.

"Probably not unique." He swirled his wine, watching the legs slide down the glass before drinking. "Life was rough, and I used to look up at the stars as a kid, wishing I was up there. I happen to be really good at stuff related to it. My brain has just always understood things like math and science. It's a language I understand."

He got quiet and looked at me over the table. I wanted to know what he was thinking, but this hooded gaze suggested secrets I wasn't ready to name. Not a road I was trying to go down.

"Tell me more about Jamal and Dr. Simone Davis," I continued, hoping to angle the conversation. He'd mentioned his mentor, Dr. Davis, and a kid he mentored named Jamal. I had met them briefly after the talk. Langston declined their offers to grab a bite and told them he had plans with me.

Langston changed the subject, turning the conversation back to me. "Enough about me. How long have you been playing music? You're talented. Too talented to be doing open mic. You professional?"

I hesitated, unsure if I wanted to delve deeper into my story. However, I still told him I played bass on tour and wrote music.

"Word?" His beautiful eyebrows lifted in surprise. "For anyone I heard of?"

Of course. Everyone has heard of that damn fool, I thought. But instead, I just said, "Maybe," and sipped on my drink.

It was clear he sensed I was holding something back, but he didn't push me to reveal more.

"Music has always been a part of me," I confessed. "It's like an extension of my soul."

We continued talking, sharing stories, and laughing. And like the first time, I found myself leaning close to him. He probably thought I couldn't hear, but it was because the tribble of his voice vibrated my kitty.

"I know it is nowhere the same as your real science and stuff. But I love sci-fi. And anime," I admitted sheepishly. "Never really tell people that. But the stories are great."

My voice trailed off as I looked over the table.

Langston grinned, his straight teeth glowing in the dim light, and suddenly we were nerding out together.

"You like Steven Universe?" he asked excitedly.

"Yes! I ship Pearl and Garnet so hard."

He laughed at how easily I used some of the show's slang.

We reached across the table to clink our glasses together.

"No one understands me either," we said in unison.

I blushed. His scent of fresh soap and spiced cologne intoxicated me as if I could taste it on my tongue.

The server asked if we needed another round, but we both declined. Langston waved him off kindly and said we should get some air.

Outside, the cool night air felt good against my skin. The stars twinkled above us, and Langston pointed out constellations like reading a book. Orion, Cassiopeia, and others. I let out a small gasp when he told me about one based on Cepheus, a mythological king of Ethiopia.

"Wow. That's the first time anyone's ever shown me that," I whispered, goosebumps prickling my arms.

He smiled. "Imagine how people used to look up at stars, see images, paint pictures." He blew out a breath in a cloud in the cold air. His nose was starting to turn red. He looked adorable. But he didn't seem to notice the cold as he looked up. "Fantasies in the sky."

He looked down at me but said nothing as he wrapped his arms around himself to stay warm.

"So, tell me about your fantasies," he murmured into the silence.

"Huh?" I blinked, caught off guard by his directness.

He chuckled. "You know, what do you like to dream about when the stars come out? What turns you on?" His voice was deep and husky, sending shivers down my spine.

"I don't know," my eyes lowered nervously. "I've never really thought about it." My cheeks warmed as I realized how naive that sounded.

"I don't think that's true," he began, taking my hand into both of his. He blew onto them, his hot breath hitting my cold skin. He flipped a hand over, and his lips, so soft, brushed against my palm.

A moment later, Langston pulled me in for a warm kiss. When our lips met, a fire ignited, spreading like wildfire through my veins. Langston's mouth moved against mine with a fervor that matched the intensity of the kiss. His lips were soft and pliant, molding perfectly to mine.

I tasted the remnants of the wine on his lips, an intoxicating blend mingling with the sweetness of his breath. His heat enveloped me, seeping into my skin. Gathering my hair peeking from under my hat, he tangled it in his fingers, willing my head back, my lips parted. His other hand slipped past my bomber jacket, onto my butt, pulling me closer.

A moan escaped me instinctually. It was all he needed to pull me in further, his tongue exploring my mouth.

My yoni pulsed, feeling his hardness press against me.

"God damn it," he said, pulling away, searching my eyes as I searched his back for answers to unasked questions.

"I think- I think I should head home." I took wobbly steps back, cold air rushing between us. I did not come to Chicago for this - it was the last thing I needed.

I waved briefly and left him confused on the cold Chicago street. And if he felt only a pinch of what I did, I also left him horny as hell.

Langston

I was lying on my bed thinking about Aurora. That's exactly what I'd been doing for the last week, ever since she left me on the cold sidewalk with an aching hard-on. If we weren't together, she filled my head anyway—obsessively. And right now, I was imagining how soft her lips were.

I groaned and shifted on the bed, moving my sweat pants that were being strained as my bulge got bigger thinking about her. That voice. That skin. That hidden tattoo. Them hips.

I closed my eyes and imagined her right on top of me. Grinding. Moaning.

I'd fuck the shit out of her.

"Simp," I snapped about myself, rolling over. I'd been decades out of high school, but still on that high school shit. Wet dreaming about the popular girl.

But Aurora wasn't anything like those popular girls I'd known. She had depth, a darkness lurking beneath her vibrant exterior that I longed to unravel. It wasn't just about physical attraction; it was about the connection we shared during that kiss. The way her body responded to mine as if it were seeking solace amid chaos.

And yet, despite the undeniable chemistry between us, she was pulling away. She'd called me the day after our kiss on the street and had made it clear on the phone that she didn't want a relationship. Hell, she didn't even want a fuck-buddy. Her words echoed in my mind: "I've been hurt before, Langston. I can't go through that again."

Marcus, the ex-boyfriend whom she had worked with. She didn't give any details beyond that he cheated. I wondered what kind of person could hurt someone like Aurora, cause whatever was going on there was more than a case of a nigga cheating.

And because of whatever he'd done, I was relegated to the "friend zone." I hadn't been friend-zoned since before I went to college, and those early years when I still looked like a boy. But then my body changed, my voice dropped, and apparently I grew into something worth looking at. Then, I got a big-time science award that put my name into circulation and got me some recognition. I went from a nobody and nothing at high school to groupie chicks literally sucking my dick at 15. Oh yeah, nerds got groupies too. Smart got them wetter than money ever did—and babygirls lined up just to crack this code. Finding an IQ as big as mine, in a body like mine, with a dick as big as mine, was apparently rare. So rare that I rarely had to look far for a fuck.

But with Aurora, I'm back to the guy who just hung out, talked, and listened. All things I wanted to do with her--between fucking.

I decided to get up, shower, and then head to the local invite-only club many of my colleagues attended. I was sure to find a groupie willing to relieve my tension. Right before I stood up, my phone vibrated. I rolled over and looked at a text.

"Wyd? Wanna hang? Live music. I'll buy. ::prayer emoji:: Please?"

It was followed by a selfie she'd taken, angled down. I saw a peak of that tattoo, glossed lips, twinkling eyes, and her full breast pushed together, looking all too fuckable.

"Shiitt!" I yelled and headed to the bathroom to get ready. Wasn't no way I was letting her walk around looking like that without me.

Chapter 4

Aurora

The melody of the song still clung to the air, notes dissipating like mist as I set down my bass. I leaned it gently against the wall of the living room. I was staying at a separate apartment on Aunt Cecily's property. She kept it for visiting artists, but she was letting me use it now while I needed a quiet, private space to sort things out. It had become my refuge, a place I could relax. And yet, now it was also the stage for an internal battle I wasn't sure I wanted to win.

"Your music... it's haunting," Langston said, his voice a warm baritone that seemed to wrap around me in a comforting embrace. I caught the gleam of admiration in his eyes, a look that made my insides flutter against my will.

"Thank you." I tucked a stray curl behind my ear. The movement was habitual, a shield to hide my embarrassment. It was silly, really, how a simple compliment from him made me feel so seen.

I sank into the plush cushions of the couch and Langston took a seat opposite. His gaze was pulling me into an orbit equal parts magnetic and terrifying.

"Langston," I began shakily, "I need to keep things... uncomplicated."

He nodded a gesture that carried the weight of understanding and something else—restraint? It was evident in how his hands, those strong, capable hands that could explain the mysteries of the universe, now sat quietly folded in his lap, he was trying to exercise self-control.

My heart ached with knowing what I was asking of us both. To remain distant when every shared glance and accidental touch screamed for closeness was torture. My past was littered with broken promises and shattered trust; I couldn't afford to collect more pieces.

"Independence is important to you," he acknowledged, his voice a velvet caress that unraveled the knots in my stomach. "And I respect that."

"More than important," I corrected, closing my eyes as if to shut out the possibility of his persuasion. "It's necessary. My heart has too many bruises already."

I opened my eyes to find him leaning forward, elbows on knees, his expression earnest. "I would never intentionally hurt you, Aurora. You must know that."

"Intention isn't always the issue, though, is it?".

There was a pause when the air seemed to hold its breath. Then Langston stood, crossing the room in a few strides to stand by the window. He looked out, perhaps at the city lights or maybe beyond, to the celestial bodies that were his constant companions. I watched him, my eyes lingering on the taut line of his shoulders. Even under the sweater he wore, I could tell he'd cared for all of his body's muscles, not just his mind. he knit of his sweater hinted at a body built for both patience and power.

"Sometimes, Aurora," he said, turning back to face me, "the risk is worth the possibility of something extraordinary."

His words lingered in the air, a challenge, a promise. I let out a slow breath, feeling the pull of desire, the yearning for connection. But still, I held fast to my defenses, knowing that the fall from such heights might leave me broken beyond repair.

When I didn't respond, Langston offered me a small, understanding smile before returning to sit down.

He looked silently at me a moment longer than I was comfortable with. "We should get to the planetarium to make that last show."

"Tell me, Aurora," Langston began, as we sat on a bench outside the planetarium, "do you know why I love astronomy so much?"

I turned to him, his profile silhouetted against the dusky sky, the first stars beginning to pierce the twilight. "I think it's because... it's infinite, right? Like your passion has no end."

"Close," he chuckled, "but not quite. It's the stories, Aurora. Every star, every constellation has its narrative, spanning across time and space."

As he spoke, something within me shifted. I listened intently as Langston pointed upwards.

"Take Orion," he said, tracing the familiar shape in the air. "In Greek mythology, he was a great hunter. But look closer, see how the three stars of his belt align so neatly? It's like they were placed there for our wonderment."

"Or maybe," I mused, allowing myself to be drawn in, "they were put there to remind us that we're part of something bigger. That our stories are connected like those stars."

"Exactly," Langston replied with a warm smile. His gaze met mine, and I swear I saw galaxies unfold in the depths of his eyes.

We walked into the planetarium, the hush of the entrance giving way to the grand dome above. The room darkened as we took our seats, and a universe of stars blossomed overhead. I gasped lightly, the expanse of the simulated night sky stretching infinitely above.

"Isn't it incredible?" Langston whispered, leaning close enough that his breath tickled my ear. "Every point of light is a sun, a star, a world, a possibility."

I nodded, entranced. Comets trailed stardust across the darkness and nebulae glowed with the colors of sunset and dawn entwined. The constellations emerged individually, each announced with a story that Langston would quietly supplement with his own commentary, a private narration for me alone. The heat of his breath on my neck caused the hairs to rise as he hushed secrets of the galaxy.

"Look, Aurora," he murmured as the constellation of Lyra appeared, "that's where the star Vega resides—one of the brightest in our night sky. In summer, it almost seems to watch over us."

"Like a guardian?"

The crowd gasped above us as Vega flickered. He traced its light on my palm instead of answering.

The show continued, a dance of light and shadow, history and science blending seamlessly. I found myself leaning towards Langston, curling close to his large presence. We shared this moment, this slice of eternity, and it was as if the walls around my heart began to crumble, unable to withstand the cosmic beauty we witnessed together.

As the presentation reached its climax, a simulation of the Milky Way spun majestically above us. I felt small yet significant, a paradox only the vastness of the universe could inspire. I risked a glance at Langston, his features bathed in starlight.

"Langston, thank you for sharing this with me. For showing me your universe."

His hand found mine in the dim light, a simple touch that spoke volumes. "Thank you, Aurora," he said, "for being willing to explore it with me."

The lights gradually returned, pulling us back to Earth, but the stars we'd witnessed seemed to linger in our eyes. As we left the planetarium, the night welcomed us back.

I'd be lying if I said I was disappointed when Langston put out his arm in a gentlemanly gesture, smiled, and said, "I better get you back. I have a class in the morning, so let's make it an early night."

The afternoon sunlight filtered through the stained glass windows of Aunt Cecily's sculpting studio, casting a kaleidoscope of colors over the clay and marble figures that stood like silent guardians around the room. I watched Langston from under my lashes as he studied one of Aunt Cecily's latest works, his hand hovering above the sculpture, almost but not quite touching.

"Your aunt is really gifted," his voice was a low hum that resonated in the quiet space. "There's so much emotion captured in these forms. Metal, stone, and clay to emotion. It's crazy."

"Her art comes from a deep place," I replied, my gaze lingering on the curve of his jaw, admiring how the light accentuated the strength there. I couldn't help wondering how the hair that graced that jaw would feel in my hands. I caught myself and looked away, focusing on a lump of untouched clay waiting on the workbench as if it held all the answers to my tumultuous thoughts.

"Much like your music," he observed, facing me. His face was a mask of unreadable emotion.

I shrugged, the room seemed to grow warmer, the air charged with an unspoken connection.

"Would you like to try?" Aunt Cecily's voice broke into the bubble, her presence unnoticed until now. She'd left to grab a tea after she'd let Langston into her studio. That, or it was her weak excuse to give us a few minutes alone. She gestured towards the clay with an encouraging smile.

"Uh, I—" I began, hesitant. The art my fingers made involved strings, not clay.

"Come on," Langston encouraged, nodding towards the workbench. "Let's make something together."

Our fingers brushed as we both reached for the clay, and it sent a jolt of electricity through my body. As Langston moved behind me, surrounding my body with his, my heart raced, betraying any attempt at maintaining composure. His hard body pressed against me, his masculine scent igniting my senses while stirring an insatiable hunger deep within my core. The brush of his fingers against mine sent fiery waves of desire coursing through my veins.

His gentle and deliberate touch guided my hands to mold the pliable earth.

"Feel the clay," Aunt Cecily instructed mildly. "Let it take shape beneath your fingertips. What it wants to be is already there. You have to let it become what it wants to be."

Our hands moved in unison, shaping and smoothing the material as we lost ourselves in creation. His biceps flexed subtly under his shirt as he leaned in closer, his breath warm against the nape of my neck. The mere contact sent ripples of need through me as my nipples tingled and my breast awoke to the desire to be the clay in Langston's hands--for him to knead and mold me.

I was aware the moment my defenses crumbled like the discarded pieces of clay that fell away from our joined efforts. Aunt Cecily watched us with a hint of mischief in her eye. She'd been saying for months I needed to open myself up again.

"Trust in the process, my dears," Aunt Cecily advised, her voice warm and nurturing. "In art, as in love, we must be fearless."

Despite myself, I looked back and met Langston's eyes. His gaze sharpened—was that longing or curiosity?—before he turned back to the sculpture.

"Are you fearless, Aurora?" Langston whispered, his question layered with meaning.

"I'm learning to be," I whispered back, my insides quivering with the effort to maintain control.

He smiled. There was a promise in that smile, a glimpse of something worth braving any storm.

We continued to work the clay, molding it into something that resembled a cross between a traditional-looking 5-point star and a starfish. Langston had slowly closed the gap between us until he molded to my backside, only a few layers of cloth between his strong erection and my ass. And though we did not speak, volumes were exchanged in shared glances and quiet laughter.

Aunt Cecily left us to our work, her departure as silent as her arrival. The studio became our world. The clay star hardened between us—imperfect edges softened by shared fingerprints.

Langston

The studio's heat clung to my skin as I stepped into the knife-edged autumn air. I could still feel how easily she'd molded against me during our sculpting session—clay forgotten.

I'd stepped away from her the moment I realized I'd begun rocking forward involuntarily, allowing my length to nestle against her soft bottom. She hadn't pulled away. I smelled the coconut scent wafting off her hair and stroked her smooth, strong fingers more than the clay.

Fool. Just torturing yourself.

I'd made an excuse about having to work early and left before I did something I'd regret.

Now, out in the street, I pulled my clothing tighter to keep out the cold air. She'd insisted on walking with me. I wish she hadn't. The streetlights cast a soft glow, creating halos on the damp pavement.

"Beautiful night," Aurora said, her voice carrying a melody.

"Every night is beautiful when you're looking at the stars," I replied, attempting to steady my voice, which threatened to reveal the tremors caused by her proximity.

We walked side by side with only inches separating us that may as well been a chasm. I wanted to close it—to reach for her hand and confirm if it would fit perfectly in mine. I hesitated, trapped by the drumbeat pulse in my throat that warned I'd crack this fragile thing that was unfolding between us.

"Can you show me Orion again?" Aurora asked, tilting her head up towards the cosmos. Walking through the park meant it was darker. And less street light meant we could see stars more clearly.

I traced the invisible line midair, fingers trembling slightly. "There—the hunter's defiant stride." Her breath hitched as she followed my gesture.

"Ah, yes, I see it now," she murmured. Her shoulder brushed against my arm, sending a current through my body.

"Orion is one of the most conspicuous constellations," I continued, trying to focus on facts instead of our proximity. "It's visible throughout the world, a constant presence."

"Like you," Aurora said, turning her eyes from the stars to meet mine.

I caught my breath as desires I had kept neatly compartmentalized spilled over, blurring lines I had drawn so carefully.

"Maybe," I managed to say, my gaze lingering on her lips before I forced it away. "But I'm not as steadfast as the stars. They don't have to contend with the gravity issue I have."

"Is that what I am to you? Gravity?" Aurora's eyes held mine, searching, questioning.

"You're perihelion—the point where orbits fray." The words left my mouth before I could rein them in, truths wrapped in astronomical metaphors.

Aurora laughed. "Well, Professor Wilkerson, your knowledge of the stars always brings me back to Earth."

"Good, because that's where I need you to be—here with me."

Silence enveloped us as we continued walking, the unspoken tension thick enough to be its own entity. My thoughts raced, each one colliding with the next. I wanted to express the depth of my feelings, to let the damn break, and confess all that I yearned for. Yet, the fear of overwhelming Aurora kept me silent.

"Langston?"

"Yes?"

"Thank you for tonight. For sharing this... and for being patient with me."

"Always, Aurora," I assured her, promising more to myself than to her. "For you, I have all the patience in the universe."

The small smile she gave me then was like a star going supernova—it outshone everything else and imprinted itself in my memory.

Aurora

I found myself in Malcolm's cozy basement studio, enveloped in a symphony of laughter and playful banter. One-quarter lay behind soundproof glass for recording; half sprawled with instruments and gear; the final quarter? A shrine to gaming decadence.

And even though Langston had brought me to see Malcolm's DIY studio, it had quickly turned into a gaming session. I sat back on the leather sofa against the wall, watching the two dueling on an old gaming system, their hands and eyes fixated on working together to send pixelated hellfire tearing through extraterrestrial battalions. Their synergy radiated nostalgia—years of inside jokes and sibling-like rivalry condensed into this basement.

"Girl, you have this scrub winning intergalactic battles to impress you," Malcolm teased, pulling the joystick to the right with all his might. A moment later, his ship burst into digital confetti, and he threw the remote down in mock frustration. I laughed, and he hopped up and embraced me.

I'd only known him for a few weeks, but it was obvious that Malcolm was a great guy. It was clear why he and Langston were friends.

His voice was rich with mirth, his locs bouncing as he shook his head at Langston. "I've never seen him fly so good."

Langston's practiced eye-roll dissolved midway as dimples cratered his cheeks. "Dust you daily," he lied through teeth fighting a grin.

"Am I, though?" Malcolm challenged. " 'cause two days ago I beat the breaks off you cause you were too busy checking your phone to see if your *star* had called you."

He rolled 'star' across his tongue like honeyed whiskey.

I cast a look at Langston, who smirked and stretched. He gave me a wink that sent flutters from my stomach to my yoni.

"Well, you are a star," Langston said, standing and striding toward me. My breath hitched, thinking he was about to kiss me. Our brief moments of contact--the heat of his palm grazing my neck yesterday or when our knees brushing under tables--rewired neural pathways primed for combustion.. It was as if we both thought that if we touched each other, if we *really* touched each other, we wouldn't stop.

"Alright, lovebirds, let's focus. Done wasted too much time. We've got work to do," Malcolm interjected, defusing the moment with his characteristic lightness. He gestured toward the instruments arrayed around. "But seriously, Aurora, your voice is going to shake the world. Thanks for agreeing to lay down a couple of lines for my project."

Malcolm had explained he was producing an experimental album with spoken word poetry, instrumentals, and a few tracks that needed a sprinkle of female vocals. While I might have been trying to avoid public attention these days, music was in my blood, so I was excited to be in a studio.

As Malcolm adjusted the sound system, Langston leaned in closer.

"Malcolm's right, you know," Langston said, standing close enough for me to notice the faint scent of sandalwood on his skin. "Your voice—" His gaze dropped to my throat. "- rewrites physics when you sing."

"Thank you," I whispered, feeling a vulnerability that crept in every time he complimented my music. "And thank you for being here, for listening..."

And that private memory burned hotter than any studio spotlight.

Langston

In the muted light of the studio, surrounded by the relics of countless gaming sessions and memories of watching my best friend experiment with sound, I had a sense of grounding I rarely experienced. Here amidst the clutter of musical aspirations, I almost believed the disparate facets of my life were aligning.

I could play. I'd been made to take music in my early years. And music, in a way, was a language of math. But it was more than that, and I could never get that extra something that turned notes into music. I was nowhere near as good as Malcolm. But I got put to work because I was hanging out in a music studio.

"Your boy here," Malcolm said, sweeping a hand toward me, "has been philosophizing about quantum jazz—rules versus improv."

"Is that so?" Aurora asked, eyes alight with curiosity that beckoned me to share more.

"Something like that," I admitted, a rush of excitement at her engagement. "There's a harmony in the chaos of the universe that resonates with the way music connects us. Especially jazz. Chaotic harmony."

"Jazz? Really?" she sounded surprised.

"It's like particles, waves, celestial bodies--from a distance, it can look chaotic. Like any minute, those stars will spin out of control. Or planets are on a collision course. But they aren't. It's a perfect symphony."

She smiled. "Sounds like both music and stars are about connection," Aurora mused, her words threading through the air. "Finding patterns and meaning in the noise."

"Exactly," I agreed. "It's about discovering where we fit in the grand scheme of things."

"Maybe," she countered gently, "it's not just about fitting in. Maybe it's also about creating our own space within it."

Her words lingered, unraveling possibilities I hadn't considered. With her, it seemed possible to carve out a niche where I belonged, to find harmony in the melding of our distinct melodies.

"Creating our own space. I like the sound of that."

Aurora

The evening breeze carried the scent of jasmine and city smoke as I walked beside Langston, my heart a steady drumline syncing with the pulse of downtown's nightlife. We'd left the laughter and warmth of Malcolm's apartment behind, but the echo of his supportive words still resonated within me. He'd been so happy with the result of my recorded voice layered with this project. I had to admit that the rough draft I heard sounded fire. We'd left him to fine-tune it.

"Beautiful night," Langston remarked, pointing upward. His hand brushed against mine. That glancing contact rippled through me like guitar feedback - sudden, primal, reverberating between us. The stars burned cold above us - celestial voyeurs of our sidewalk tango.

"Every time I look up now, I see more than just lights," I said, my voice a soft confession. "I see stories, constellations of life."

Langston smiled, his white teeth contrasting against the depth of his complexion in the moon's silver glow. "And yet, there's so much more to show you."

Our gazes locked, and for a moment, it was as though the universe had shrunk down to the space between us.

"Like what?" I asked, tilting my head, aware of how my hair cascaded over one shoulder.

"Let's save some mysteries for another night," he replied, his voice low and teasing, tugging at the hem of intrigue that dressed our encounter.

We continued walking, our bodies occasionally grazing one another as we navigated through the crowded sidewalk. Each touch was like a note held a beat too long, stirring harmonies within that threatened to break into melody.

"Your Aunt Cecily," Langston began, redirecting my thoughts, "she mentioned a sculpture she's working on. A duet between two forms."

I felt a ridiculous flutter beneath my ribs - why did pavement cracks suddenly feel electrified at his proximity? "Two different elements coming together to create something new. She didn't tell me what it was. It's covered in the back of the studio."

There was a moment of silence.

"Sometimes, there is a tension in our conversations," Langston admitted, careful to keep his voice even. "Like we're both holding back an energy that wants to fuse together."

I stopped breathing for a moment, the honesty in his words hit me in the stomach.

"Energy can be... overwhelming," I managed to say, my fingers itching to reach out, to trace the lines of his jaw that clenched ever so slightly when he was deep in thought.

"Overwhelming, yes," he agreed, pausing to let his gaze drift from my eyes down to my lips and back again. "But also illuminating."

"Langston, sometimes I think you see right through me."

"Only because you let me," he responded, his voice husky with subtext.

We arrived at the entrance of my place, and I was a bit sad. The doorway signaled where we'd part.

"Goodnight, Aurora," he said, his hand lingering in a ghostly caress as he withdrew from our almost-touch.

"Goodnight, Langston," I echoed, the weight of the unsung chorus between us, heavy with notes of what-could-be. I watched him turn to walk away into the night when I called after him.

"Langston, wait. Why don't you come in for a drink."

Under the dim glow of the streetlight, Langston turned back, his expression a canvas of restrained yearning brushed with surprise. "Are you sure?" he asked, the gravity in his voice betraying the careful balance we had maintained.

My heart thrummed a bold, erratic beat. "Yes," I said, unlocking the door to the mother-in-law suite nestled within Aunt Cecily's urban oasis. The space was an intimate cocoon, separate from the main house, imbued with the same eclectic charm that marked all of Cecily's influence.

As Langston stepped inside, I sensed the shift in the air, a current charged with anticipation. I led him through the small living area to the kitchenette, where I poured each of us a glass of red wine, the rich aroma spilling into the silence.

My heart raced as I handed him the glass, allowing my fingers to brush against his briefly. Langston had taken off his coat, revealing the camel-colored knitted V-neck sweater that hung off his broad shoulders and back, drawing attention to the tantalizing curve of his clavicle. The subtle glint of a gold chain nestled against his skin emphasized the strength of his chest underneath.

"Thank you," Langston said. Our eyes met, and in that instant, the world seemed to contract until there was nothing but the space we shared.

My eyes traced the contours of his physique, a finely tuned athletic build reminiscent of some quarterbacks I'd seen on TV. Every coiled inch of him screamed NCAA rushing yards – discipline trained to please. His jeans clung to his thighs before gracefully loosening, offering a glimpse of his powerful legs. My fingers itched to touch, to explore his form's subtle ridges and valleys. His deep brown hair, neatly styled in a low fade, framed his face, while a mustache tapered down to meet a beard that had grown out just enough to be tugged on.

Langston was a captivating blend of strength and elegance, a sight to behold, and I found myself mesmerized by his presence in the space I was calling home.

"Cheers," I murmured, touching my glass to his.

"Your aunt has quite the artistic touch," he commented, setting his glass down and looking around. His gaze caught on the bass guitar propped against the wall, the strings a silent testament to my own artistry. "You've created a beautiful sanctuary here."

"Aunt Cecily and I are a lot alike. I like this place. It's a reflection of... me," I admitted, fingers tracing the stem of the wine glass. "The place, it's almost like home."

Langston walked around, sipping from his glass. His eyes landed on a picture of me at a party. I stood next to a Hispanic woman, and each of us were flanked by a tall, good-looking African American man. The one next to me had a possessive arm twisted around my waist. Langston picked up the picture frame and looked from it to me.

"Friends? You never talk about your friends."

Two strides and I had crossed the small room and plucked it out of his hands. "Not friends. People I used to work with."

Langston didn't respond, just looked at me passively. He wasn't going to press, but I could tell he didn't believe me.

I walked back over to the counter and slammed the frame face-down, drained the rest of the glass in one swoop, and poured another one.

Langston took a step forward and then stopped. "I'm sorry if I brought up something-"

"Nothing to be sorry about," I interrupted, trying to sound non-chalant. I avoided his gaze, focusing on the patterns in the wood of the counter.

Langston noticed a sketchbook lying nearby and decided to change the subject. He picked it up and flipped through the pages, admiring the intricate drawings within. "These are incredible, Aurora. You're so talented."

My late mother was an amazing sketch artist. I wasn't as good as her, but she'd taught me the basics.

"Thank you," I murmured, grateful for the distraction. The tension in my body eased a bit as I watched him admire the work.

As Langston turned another page, he came across a detailed portrait of the man from the picture... a rather intimate one I'd drawn. Langston let out a small, involuntary gasp. I looked up, panicked as I remembered the drawing. I rushed over to snatch the sketchbook from his hands.

"Sorry, you weren't meant to see that," I stammered, my face flushed with embarrassment.

"Is this...?" Langston didn't finish the question.

I nodded, finally admitting, "That's Marcus, my ex-boyfriend. I haven't had the heart to throw away some of these things yet."

A heavy silence settled between us, the unspoken memories of Marcus lingering like a dark cloud. My grip tightened on the sketchbook, and my breathing became shallow as old pains resurfaced.

Langston approached and his hand delicately rubbed my arm. "Hey," he said softly, his voice full of concern. "You don't have to explain anything to me. We all have a past."

I looked up into his warm, understanding eyes and wanted to cry. But instead, I mustered a weak smile. "Thank you, Langston. You always know what to say."

As Langston's hand moved up to rest on my shoulder, a shiver ran down my spine. His hand moved to trace the delicate bones along my shoulder blades before resting on my neck. Langston closed the space between us until our lips almost touched. The heat emanating from him was intoxicating.

"Langston," I whispered.

He leaned closer, his warm breath caressing my cheek like a feather-light kiss. Our lips brushed against each other with a hesitant tremble.

With a quivering hand, I reached up to cup his face, pulling him closer as our kiss deepened. Our tongues danced together with an urgent hunger that left us both gasping for air. The taste of his mouth was intoxicating, like fine wine and freshly brewed coffee mixed into one perfect flavor. He pressed his body harder against me, his arousal clear even through our clothes.

Langston's free hand slid around my waist, pulling me flush against his hard chest. His touch sent shockwaves of pleasure through my core as his thumb traced a slow path along the delicate curve of my hip bone. I whimpered gently into the kiss, arching into him as he gripped me tighter. Langston groan softly against my lips and all but devour them in response.

The stubble of his unshaven jaw scraped against my smooth skin, sending shivers of delight down my neck and spine.

"Aurora." My name came out gruff between heavy breaths. His lips moved away from mine, down my neck, and onto my shoulder, which he'd revealed with a rough pull at my sweater. All I could do was echo his name.

He stopped for a moment and looked at the small musical notes inked on my shoulder. He smiled and returned his lips to my body.

His hands moved under my sweater, strong and possessive. His lips didn't miss a beat as he undid my bra. My breast, now released, tingled with excitement as the cloth brushed over my nipples. Langston dropped the sweater to the ground and stared at my milk chocolate mounds.

Without a word, he took one nipple into his mouth and rolled the other between his fingers. I moaned and shivered. The sound of my voice made him look up at me. And fuck me if amusement didn't shine in his eyes as he let out a low growl.

My hands moved from the back of his neck to pulling at his sweater. I wanted to see him. I needed to see him.

A moment later, he unlatched, flicking his tongue over my nipple once more before taking off his sweater and unbuttoning the top of his jeans.

My eyes grazed over his form, a ripple of thick muscles. To my surprise the white-inked tattoo I had peeked on his forearm when he pushed up his shirt, a few scattered stars, was just the introduction to a more detailed piece that covered the top portion of one arm and expanded across part of his chest. It was the scene of a black hole that was enveloping stars. As I looked at it, I realized all the stars, including the ones on his forearm, were being drawn into it. I don't know what I imagined from the analytical hulk, but this wasn't it. The beautiful ink caught me off guard.

"Fuck me," I whispered in admiration, my eyes dancing across his body.

"Oh, I plan too." Langston was back on me a moment later, using his thumbs to push down my jeans to an unceremonious heap on the floor. He picked me up and placed me on the counter. Our tongues played with one another as he rubbed a hand against my warm, hot sex through my panties.

"Wet," he murmured. "Perfect."

A second later, a thick finger entered into my depths, then another. The curses that spilled from my lips only seemed to inspire Langston to push in deeper and faster.

"Oh, shit." I began moving my hips, grinding in motion to his hand, my juices beginning to move down his hand. My eyes rolled back, and my nails scratched across his back. "Don't stop."

Langston responded by dropping to his knees. He pushed my panties out of the way and his tongue replaced his fingers. I yelped in surprise, and squeezed my legs around his head.

"Relax, baby. Let me make you feel good." I could feel the heat of his mouth as he spoke. He pushed my legs apart, and let his tongue lick my clit before reentering.

His hard, warm tongue, combined with the feeling of his facial hair brushing my sensitive skin was too much. Instinctively I held his head as I began to thrust my hips, experiencing him deeper.

I shuttered before a wave of heat overtook me, and I felt a release of liquid.

"You taste so fucking good. I knew you would."

Langston stood, evidence of his hard work glistening on his mustache and beard. He bent and took a small package from the jeans on the floor. He slipped his boxers off to reveal a long shaft with a thick vein. He stood to attention as he slipped on the condom.

I licked my lips, desire pouring from me.

Langston pulled me forward on the counter, so my ass cheeks narrowly kept me on.

From the moment the tip touched my entrance, a ripple of excitement danced across my breast. Langston exhaled and looked at me a moment before slowly stretching the inside of me with his girth.

He let out a sound of raw desire as he began pulling himself out and pushing himself back in. I had to grip the sides of the counter to stay on, but I wished I could touch him. My juices still glistened in his facial hair, and I wanted to taste myself on him.

As if he understood, Langston moved in and covered my mouth with his. As I tasted my sex on his lips, Langston began moving faster, and harder.

"More," I ordered between rough kisses.

Compliant, Langston reached down and gripped my ass and lifted me up, then onto the floor. His length never exited as he moved out until the tip almost slipped. Then, with a forceful thrust, he reentered. The hard floor gave me no room for movement, and the thrust fully entered, pinning me in place.

"Fuck it, Aurora. What did you do?" He pulled out and slammed into me again and again. I sung his name, and a moment later, he jerked, his body tensed, and even through the condom, I felt him empty himself.

He let his body weight rest on me for a moment before rolling off and staring up at the ceiling. Neither of us spoke, but I loved the silence. My vagina throbbed in memory of what I'd just experienced.

I pushed onto my side and looked at him.

"Damn, Professor Wilkerson."

A smile crinkled his face, and he let a hand caress one of my breasts. We looked at each other for a moment before I gathered the strength to stand. I grabbed his hand, pulled it, and encouraged him to stand.

"We're not sleeping on the floor all night."

"What?" Langston made an exaggerated movement of surprise. "You not kicking a brother out after he gave up the ass?"

An eye roll and a swat, and I walked away, being sure to give an extra sway of the hips for his view. A few minutes later, we laid in bed, limbs twisted together, my head on his chest.

My thighs still hummed from counter-edge grip as Langston's breathing slowed and he drifted into a peaceful sleep, his arm protectively draped over me.

I gazed at his sleeping form, thoughts a whirlwind of emotions. I traced my finger over the outline of his face, marveling at how this man had managed to break down my walls and touch my soul in a way no one else ever had. Not even freaky Marcus had made me feel the way Langston had.

As I looked at Langston, I realized that our connection had reached a new level – and it scared me.

Chapter 5

Langston

My fingers drummed on the cluttered desk in time with distant raindrops fingering glass. I glanced up at Dr. Simone Davis, who sat, her piercing blue eyes studying me. She always had a way of making me feel exposed. I was never really good at hiding things from her.

Even though I had a myriad of accomplishments now, when I was starting out no one was jumping up to mentor an inner-city black kid who had the vibrato to say he wanted to get a Nobel one day. No one except Dr. Davis, who was about 30 years my senior. She said as a woman in astrophysics, she understood what it was like to be outside in the very tight-knit, somewhat homogeneous community. She wore academia's scars like pearls - entry wounds from shattering glass ceilings now strung into ladders. And she was one of the first ones willing to drop down one of those ladders for me.

"I think the results of your last tests and the calculations you made are fantastic. I really think you should submit your findings to the committee and see if they'll approve the next phase. I have a few experts in mind we might be able to get to come in on the project... Langston, are you even listening?" she asked, her voice soft but stern.

"Sorry," I mumbled, forcing my focus back to our conversation. It had been a few days since my passionate rendezvous with Aurora, and the memory of her touch still lingered, distracting me from the present moment. I usually had some new ideas to run by Dr. Davis a few times a week. I hadn't spoken to her in two weeks before today.

She sighed, leaning back in her chair and folding her arms across her chest. "You've been off lately. Is everything okay?"

"Everything's fine," I replied, forcing a smile. The intensity of my connection with Aurora had seeped into every corner of my mind, clouding my thoughts and making it difficult to concentrate on anything else.

"Langston, I've known you for years. You can't fool me," she said, concern etched upon her face. "Ever since that woman started visiting campus, you've been different. Good, but different. Good, but unfocused."

I shifted uncomfortably in my seat, suddenly very aware of the weight of her gaze. "Her name's Aurora," I said quietly. "She's... well, she's something special."

"Clearly," Dr. Davis replied, her expression softening as she regarded me with a knowing look. "It's good to see you happy, Langston. Just don't forget about your work and your students."

"Of course not," I said, fully aware that balancing personal and professional lives would be a struggle. Before Aurora, I had sex that didn't interfere with my focus. A quick fuck with a casual acquaintance wasn't distracting. But this was different. My distraction had already made me feel that of late I'd given less to my students. As if on cue, a knock at the door interrupted our conversation.

"Come in," I called, grateful for something to pull me out of my thoughts.

"Professor Wilkerson?" Jamal poked his head into the office, his eyes wide with urgency. "I need to speak with you. It's important."

"Of course," I replied, nodding towards Dr. Davis. "I'll catch up with you later?"

Dr. Davis glanced between Jamal and me before standing up. "I'll leave you two to it," she said with a smile. "Don't forget about submitting your findings, Langston. And remember, it's okay to have a life outside work." With that, she walked out, closing the door behind her.

"Take a seat, Jamal." I gestured to the chair Dr. Davis had vacated. "What's on your mind?"

Jamal hesitated before sitting down, his face etched with worry. "I... I might have to drop out of the program, Professor," he admitted, his voice scarcely above a whisper.

My heart sank at the news. I studied the young man before me—there was so much of me in Jamal. We shared the same passion for learning, the same desire to make a difference, and the same struggle with the pressures of our community. I appreciated how important it was for me to be there for Jamal, like others had been there for me when I was younger.

"Why?" I asked, trying to keep the concern out of my voice.

Jamal hesitated, swallowing hard. "My family needs me to work, and they don't understand why this science is so important to me. My mom's been sick, and we're drowning in medical bills. They need a bit of another income in the house while she recovers. I'm young, but I did graduate high school. I *can* work... I don't know if I can afford to stay in school."

I remember facing similar challenges in my life, trying to balance my dreams and aspirations with the expectations placed upon me by my family. I can still remember the confusion and irritation on the face of a cousin who didn't understand why a 10-year-old boy wanted to go to summer camp on a college campus more than make a few bucks doing odd jobs.

"Jamal, you have a unique mind. You're passionate about the sciences, and you have so much potential. Let me see if there's something I can do to help you find a solution. Don't give up on your dreams yet."

The young man looked up, tears brimming in his eyes. "I appreciate that, Professor, but I don't see any other option."

"Let me help you find a solution," I urged him. "Give me until the end of the semester before making a final decision. We'll figure something out."

"Thank you," Jamal whispered, his voice wavering as he nodded. "I'll... I'll wait."

As Jamal left the office, I couldn't help but feel overwhelmed by the weight of responsibility I carried – for my students, my research, and now for Aurora. Something was off with her. My thoughts were interrupted by the buzzing of my phone. It was Malcolm.

"Hey, man, you need to check your text messages and call me back as soon as you can," Malcolm's voice was urgent, causing my heart to race.

"Alright," I replied, hanging up and pulling up Malcolm's messages. My stomach dropped as I read the first headline and looked at the picture:

"Marcus James dishes dirt on dirty Ex."

Under it was a picture of Aurora attempting to avoid being in a paparazzi picture.

I clicked on a video link that showed a suave-looking man with his hair cut into a curly frohawk. He wore a red leather jacket and too much jewelry. I recognized him from the picture and drawing at Aurora's place. I had no idea who he was, but I already hated him.

"You know where she at?" the man began. The video looked like it was from the man's social media posting. "I'm here, making my music. Doing what I always did. Went ahead and replaced her cause she replaceable. And where she at? Disappeared. Some lying chick ain't gonna stop me. I'm out here telling y'all the truth, and she gone. She saying I stole her music--but who is she? Y'all ain't never heard of her, and all of sudden she say she's the one. Nah."

My stomach turned, and I clicked another link. It was a short article on a gossip column about upcoming star Marcus James being sued by an unnamed female claiming she wrote most of his album.

Unnamed. I huffed. Aurora. Why hadn't she mentioned any of this? While I might not be up on the latest music, whoever this Marcus character was, this was apparently a big thing.

The memory of the pain on Aurora's face when I'd found that picture of Marcus, her reluctance to play or sing in public, how ill-at-ease she seemed at Malcolm's studio, it came flooding back. I couldn't sit here like a crazy person wondering why a woman I had only known for a few weeks didn't tell me all her business. If just a piece of me might care for her, I knew that was a shitty selfish response. I needed to find her and make sure she was okay.

I grabbed my coat, left everything unfinished on my desk, and went out to find her.

Jamal's words still echoed as I hurried across the campus. I knew she needed me now more than ever.

As I reached the edge of the campus where my car was parked, I pulled out my phone and dialed Malcolm. The phone rang once before Malcolm's voice came through, tense and worried.

"Langston, man, did you see those videos? Do you know who he is? No, of course you don't cause you still don't listen to anything that dropped after 2017."

I suck my teeth. Malcolm always got jokes.

"Seriously though," Malcolm 's voice shifted to a somber tone. "He up and coming. Voiced for recent few top rap songs, the singing vocals. Went from being a music influencer on social media, singing original stuff, to about to drop a hot album soon. His first single is going really good right now. He's a name all *normal people* would know. And he's her ex? And that guy's trying to destroy her. Did you see those videos? " Malcolm said, anger dripping from his voice.

"Yeah, I saw them. I'm on my way to find her now. Do you know where she might be? I called her, no answer." I tried to steady a rush of adrenaline from the information dump I'd received. I certainly wasn't up on the latest influencers, but I knew enough to realize the guy sounded like he had some power in her world.

"Check Aunt Cecily's. She might've gone there," Malcolm suggested.

"Thanks, Malcolm. I'll let you know if I find her."

"Good luck, man. Be there for her. She needs someone like you right now," Malcolm said before hanging up the phone.

I quickened my pace, my heart thumping wildly in my chest. Arriving at Aunt Cecily's studio, I hesitated momentarily outside the door, took a deep breath, and knocked. The door creaked open, revealing a distressed Aurora. Her eyes were red and puffy from crying, and she clutched a bunch of papers in her trembling hands.

Aurora

It had been a good morning. Thoughts of Langston had me thinking positively for the first time in a while. I even wanted to pick up my bass and develop a few new lyrics to contribute to Malcolm's project. And like clockwork, there was Marcus again. It was as if he could smell my happiness. When a former bandmate sent me the links earlier today, I almost didn't click on them. Now I wished I hadn't.

"Aurora, it's going to be OK." As always, Aunt Cecily had been a rock. "You know he is an ass, so when the summons was served, this is to be expected. A whole media circus by him magically starts at the same time his counter-suit is filed. It doesn't matter what he says, this isn't a trial by media."

All I could do was shake my head. It was different for Aunt Cecily--the court of public opinion couldn't easily ruin an artist like her. Gossip about the personal life of an established amazing artist probably won't affect their sales, unless they did something really bad... But a musician like me, one who didn't even have a name yet to ruin--this could end my dream before it began.

Fandom tribunals moved faster than tour buses - one viral thread could shred a career before the coffee went cold. Even if I won the lawsuit proving I was technically right, but the public was left hating me, I'd lost. Who'd ever sign me as a potential serious artist with that negative chaos tied to me publicly?

"I should have expected it, but still... how could he say these things after all we went through? After everything he knows I did for him-!"

A sob choked off my last words. A soothing hand rubbed my back before Aunt Cecily embraced me.

I looked down at the notice of countersuit from Marcus' lawyer that had arrived just before the links had. The back-and-forth legal action wasn't something I wanted, but I had started it--Marcus hadn't given me any options.

When I began dating Marcus in my freshman year of college, the two of us had big dreams. Two aspiring artists whose dreams seem to complement one another. Marcus had the voice, the looks, the presence. And me? I had the music. And I was completely happy writing those songs, those bangers, those lines, and playing in the background. I was on the stage, and that was enough for me. And when he looked over his shoulder as he sang and gave a conspiratorial, flirtatious wink, it was to me, the woman he'd called the love of his life. And for a long time, I believed it was perfect.

The truth burned - I'd only ever seen reflections of my own hopes. He wasn't looking at me at all. He'd been mining my melodies like coal - all heat and no light left for me.

"Why don't you put that down." Aunt Cecily's voice brought me back to the moment. She took the letter out of my hand and placed it on the table. "Of course, you can stay here with me today. The reporters haven't found out you are staying with me. But I think you should call Langston."

His name snapped my attention upward to Aunt Cecily's knowing smile.

"He's good medicine for you, girl."

I hesitated, my fingers hovering over the screen of the phone. Langston had been a tremendous source of comfort and support in my life lately, but I felt like a burden to him. He seemed fairly private, and I doubt he'd welcome this insanity. But Aunt Cecily was right; I needed someone.

"Alright, I'll call him."

"Good," Aunt Cecily replied, giving my shoulder a reassuring squeeze before leaving me to make the call.

As soon as my Aunt left, my finger froze. The thought of trusting another man with any of my real feelings... I couldn't do it. Plus, if Langston had heard any of the stuff floating around online today, he'd probably be putting as much distance between us as possible.

So I sat in the quiet studio, allowing my thoughts to race. The memories of my time with Marcus haunted me, making me question my own worth and talent. *Maybe I was the villain in this story? Had I brought this on myself?*

But when I heard a knock on Aunt Cecily's studio door, and opened it to find Langston on the other side, all those doubts vanished. Concern and worry were etched on his face. It was as if he gave permission for me to let go as he hugged me close. I allowed myself to break down, letting him hold me as sobs wracked my body.

"Everything will be alright," Langston whispered into my ear, followed by a soft kiss on my temple.

Aunt Cecily had come back when she heard the knock. She stood back and let Langston hold me as I cried.

"He is trying to sway public opinion before the court date," Aunt Cecily explained, trying to offer some clarity amidst the chaos. "He's scared of what she might say or do, so Marcus is attempting to discredit her first."

My face buried in Langston's chest, my thoughts drifted back to my relationship with Marcus. We had been inseparable, once upon a time. I had poured my heart and soul into our shared music. It was devastating to think that the man I had loved and trusted would stoop so low as to steal my work and tarnish my reputation.

"He's just afraid, honey," Aunt Cecily continued, this time addressing me. "But you can't let his fear dictate your life. You're stronger than that, and you have more talent in one finger than he has in his entire being."

I took a deep breath and wrapped my arms around Langston, focusing on the warmth of his body against mine. My aunt was right. I couldn't let Marcus win by succumbing to his manipulations. I had fought too hard for my dreams and had come too far to give up now.

"Thank you, Aunt Cecily. And thank you, Langston. I don't know what I'd do without you two."

About an hour later, I was sitting on a stool in the studio. Langston's voice could be heard in the other room. He and Aunt Cecily were making tea and talking. The private moment let my mind drift back to when I was truly in love with Marcus. I remembered how he made me feel like I was the only person in the world who mattered. He was good at that--making other people feel good. Our jam sessions always climaxed the same way - tangled cords, sheet music confetti, and his teeth marking quarter-note bruises on my thighs. And I thought life was good then. It seemed like a lifetime ago, but the memories still lingered, both sweet and bitter.

The bitter part of those memories flooded my thoughts as I recalled the day of Marcus' betrayal, his lies, couldn't be covered over. I remember how he flipped it back on me, though I still don't know how he'd done that--how he turned me into the villain. I pictured the anger in his eyes as he kicked me out of our shared apartment, telling me that my career was finished. He had been so cold, so cruel, and it was a side of him I had never seen before. But maybe I had seen it, but I ignored it? The truth is that once I started writing the songs, Marcus had managed to go from a social media nobody to an international name in a short time. I'd ignored the people who said he was a selfish, manipulative dick, assigning it to them being jealous. In fact, I'd ignored a lot about him that now if I looked back, and was honest, I realized it had to be there. I was getting what I wanted--my music heard. I chose not to really listen to what people were saying.

I ignored it until the day I couldn't. That man had left me broken and unsure if I'd ever be able to pick up the pieces of my shattered life.

Now, as I faced the prospect of taking Marcus to court and fighting him in the media, I couldn't help but wonder if I had the strength to do it. *Could I really stand up to the man who had once meant everything to me?* After years of him picking away at me, telling me I was nothing without him... while it might not have been true when we got together, I was scared that it might be true now.

Aunt Cecily and Langston reentered. She was familiar with the look on my face, and aware I must be mentally beating myself up.

"Remember, honey," Aunt Cecily said gently, sliding into a seat in front of me. "You are not alone in this fight. You got receipts that he don't want you to pull in public."

"Your passion is what drew me to you in the first place," Langston added. "Don't let this Marcus character take that away from you."

I nodded, drawing confidence from their unwavering support. They were right. I couldn't let Marcus' betrayal define me or dictate my future.

Later that day I sat on the edge of my bed, cradling my head in my hands as the weight of Marcus' accusations bore down on me. It was so easy in theory to be strong, but in reality, I was in a cycle of self doubt. Marcus' damaging rumors had spread like wildfire across social media, tarnishing my budding reputation and staining my once-promising career. The social media fray scrolled behind my eyelids each time I blinked awake - every comment section a fresh bruise.

"Look at me," Aunt Cecily's voice broke through my haze of despair. "You can't let him win, Aurora. You can't let Marcus destroy everything you've worked so hard for."

I lifted my tear-streaked face to meet my aunt's determined gaze. "But it's so hard, Aunt Cecily. Everyone believes him. And he's made sure that I have no one left to turn to in the industry."

"Who cares about that now. They'll come around. That mask Marcus has will slip. But for now, you have other people who support you. Like Langston," Aunt Cecily whispered. Langston was in the kitchen making yet another pot of tea. He'd picked up on the fact that just holding a cup of warm tea, smelling the aroma, was comforting to me. "He has been good for you, hasn't he? Since breaking up with Marcus this is the first time I've seen you happy. Talk to him."

A moment later, when Langston returned with two mugs, my aunt waved him off and made excuses to leave us alone.

Realizing my aunt was right, I decided to open a crack and talk to Langston. He might not really understand all the nuances of the industry, but I needed to speak, and he was a safe place, so far away from the bull.

As the conversation continued, I allowed myself to open up to Langston, sharing my fears and doubts about fighting Marcus in court and the media. He sat quiet, not interrupting, peppering me with questions, or giving unrequested advice. He just listened.

"Thank you, Langston. I think talking helps."

"Strength isn't what you know." His thumb traced the hinge of my jaw where tension pulsed. "It's who you choose to be while drowning."

Langston

I hadn't packed any clothing to spend the night at Aurora's. In fact, I hadn't spent the night there since the first time we'd been together.

I fished in my pocket for a tip for the person who had delivered a pair of sweatpants and a t-shirt I'd ordered online. It was a cute woman with light brown skin and a spattering of freckles across her face. She smiled as I gave my ID for the alcohol that she was delivering as well. She fingered it as she punched in the date of birth, then gave me a wiry smile.

"You don't look that old."

"I am," I said, holding my hand to get the ID back.

The woman looked me up and down. I was in need of a haircut and beard trim before the shit with Aurora. It was a day later, and I was wearing the same clothes, and I knew I looked like a scruffy mess. Apparently, scruffy hot mess is what this girl liked.

Her smile broadened.

"Hitting a whole bottle of crown by yourself?" She cast a look over my shoulder. "That's no fun."

"I'll be good." I handed her the cash tip, and she gripped my hand instead of withdrawing it.

"I don't have any more app orders right now."

Before I could reply the door jerked open wider. Aurora was standing there in a robe, having just come out of the shower. She gave the woman a nasty look before snapping.

"He straight. Get your tip, get your 5-stars, and get off my doorstep."

The woman looked surprised. I was a bit surprised too, but Aurora had been in a foul mood since yesterday. She'd avoided snapping at me or her Aunt, but this lady received no such luck.

The delivery woman looked Aurora up and down, narrowed her eyes, and widened her smile.

"Sorry, no disrespect."

After the woman had left, Aurora slung the bags of food that had also arrived onto the counter. She was making tacos.

"Heffas always trying me," she muttered as she unpacked.

Wisdom told me to give her a bit of space, and I could use a minute to think as well. As I lathered up in the shower, my mind drifted back to the things Aurora had told me through tears over the last day.

It was obvious that Aurora still was keeping part of the story to herself. But I had heard enough of it and knew Aurora and her talent well enough to know two things: Aurora was most definitely the soul behind the music, and Marcus sounded like a real piece of shit.

But I could also tell that, for some reason, Aurora thought she was at fault somehow. Little phrases I caught in her story: "... I pushed him into it," "...I should have known," "...I wasn't what he needed." She even said she didn't understand why Marcus was doing all this since "he was more talented" and "better on stage."

Sounded like this nigga had gaslit her for years.

The good thing was that she had almost all the song lyrics in her handwriting and text messages showing that she worked on the songs with Marcus. The problem seemed to be proving who helped who in the process--and since she'd never asked for credit before, her sudden departure from Marcus' inner circle and his social media blitz had it looking like Aurora was just a crazy chick who was rejected, fired, and got mad. It didn't seem like two romantic partners who had a personal fallout, and all she wanted was what was hers in the split.

"I should have realized when I signed that non-disclosure," she'd cried the night before. "Something wasn't right. As soon as Marcus signed Tony as manager, then had me sign right along, the first thing that snake did was have me sign a non-disclosure about anything I knew about Marcus, including my personal relationship with him. Tony said it was to maintain an image. Single-sex symbols sell more. What an absolute load of shit, and I swallowed it whole."

No one outside the inner circle was aware Aurora and Marcus were together. She said she didn't do public events prior to Tony, and once the manager came on board, the plan was to keep Marcus looking like a player. So the public didn't know her. And those in the inner circle had signed the same non-disclosure.

So the fact that Aurora says she caught Marcus cheating wasn't something that was going to come out. And even if she broke the NDA, no one else would risk it. So she'd sound like a crazy, bitter woman with no one to back her up.

Marcus had taken her heart, her music, and her career - left her with nothing but NDAs. Even though she'd attempt to prove the malicious intent to defraud her in court within a few weeks, Aurora wasn't sure she could prove it.

She told me she'd come to Chicago to hide from the public eye until the case was heard. Lie low and heal. Instead, I had bogarted my way into her life. A happy distraction, I supposed. But a distraction... not a relationship.

She wasn't ready for that. She couldn't handle that.

I let out a sigh of frustration as I began to rinse off. The door to the shower cracked, and I looked back to see Aurora standing there, naked, smooth-skinned, with a lustful look in her eyes.

"Didn't you already shower?" I loved teasing her.

"I missed a spot." She stepped into the space that was already scarcely big enough for my large frame. Aunt Cecily did not plan this apartment to cater for guys of my size. Aurora's wet skin pressed against me immediately making my dick stand to attention.

"Aurora," I purred her name and tried to move her hand from stroking my shaft. It's not that I didn't want it.

She was fucking great.

We'd had sex about six times since we got to her apartment. Mind-blowing sex. Distraction sex. I wanted to know her deeper, how she was feeling. I wanted to know what she wasn't telling me.

And Aurora? She just wanted to fuck and not talk.

"Mhmm?" she hummed.

"I was thinking we'd go out for dinner-." Before I could finish my sentence, she was on her knees. I put my head back, letting the water from the shower hit my chest. When the tip hit the back of her throat, I looked down.

She looked like a Goddess. Her eyes were round and doe-like. Her hair dripped wet as the water hit her from behind. Her round breasts with water streaming down them might have been the picture of perfection. I gripped one of them and squeezed. So firm. She moaned but didn't take me out of her mouth.

My knees nearly buckled as she began moving her head back and forth to some amazing rhythm in her head. I put my hand in the tangle of her wet mane and guided her to suck deeper.

She gagged a bit.

"I'm sorry, baby," I said quickly, moving my hand to let her withdraw. But she didn't. She cupped my balls with one hand and took that dick down as far as she could.

"Shhiiit." I banged my head on the wall and put my hand back.

And I fucked her face until I felt that build-up. I pulled out in time to let my release spilled across her collarbone.

She licked a bit that landed near her mouth, kissed the tip of my dick, stood, and turned toward the shower head. Her juicy ass brushed against my sensitive member. I moved forward so it nestled right in the slot of her ass as I kissed her shoulder.

"Aurora, you are amazing."

She turned, smiled, and gave me a peck on the mouth, then returned to rinsing the cum off her face and neck. Our bodies spoke in languages our mouths refused - hers all sharp need drowning soft fears, mine trying to say what words couldn't carry.

We didn't talk about her feelings that day. We found each other twice more that afternoon - frantic couplings where words couldn't reach what our bodies communicated.

"Man, where have you been?"

Malcolm had snuck into the back of the lecture hall after I finished my Monday class. I hadn't spoken to him since Friday. I'd been locked in the house with Aurora all weekend, listening to her occasional incoherent rants and fucking the shit out of her on demand.

It was both a shitty and amazing weekend.

"What's good, man?" I asked as I slipped my laptop into my leather messenger bag.

"What's good?" he parroted. "Where have you been? I've been blowing up your phone. You ain't answering. You ain't home. Don't nobody know where you at-"

"I was with Aurora."

"I figured that much." He stewed for a minute, then crossed his arms, a look of concern crinkling his face. "I mean, that Marcus guy ain't my kinda artist, but game should have recognized game. I should have realized who she was."

I shrugged. Music wasn't my world, the stars were. But even I knew most people didn't know or pay attention to the people that filled the stage behind the star.

"How is she?" he asked as we walked toward the parking lot.

"Horrible," I admitted. She had refused to leave the house since Friday.

Malcolm nodded. "I read up on some of that stuff on gossip blogs and pages. Ain't too much out there, and what is out there is all Marcus. I can tell that he's on the bullshit. I know Aurora ain't the way he describes her."

"Most definitely." I sighed when we got to his old school Jeep that he'd parked alongside my car. "But she gonna be good. I mean, she gotta be right? All that dude doing is lying."

This time, it was Malcolm's turn to shrug. "Yeah, but this ain't one of them planets you studying man. This earth, and it's full of people ready to believe shit-holes like Marcus. I mean, I don't know what we can do to help, but whatever it is, you know I got y'all back."

I had to smile. Malcolm called us "y'all" like a unified couple, not two fuck buddies. And while that might be all Aurora saw us as, I wouldn't be satisfied with that. I'd had a taste, and now I wanted it all.

"For sure," I smiled, dapping up my friend. "She definitely gonna need the whole village to support her man."

Chapter 6

Aurora

"Come on, Aurora. It'll be good for you." Langston had said this phrase repeatedly once my Aunt reminded us of the Open Mic Night at the same spot we'd met at.

How could a night out, submerged in a sea of faces and unsolicited attention, be good for me? Yet something about the earnest glint in Langston's eyes—a hope, perhaps, or a quiet determination—made it hard to say no.

Or maybe it was the fact that he'd crawled on top of me, nibbling my ear, while he asked me about twenty times in a row until I relented.

We drove in silence - no need for words when the engine's hum said enough. My thoughts swirled. It was the first time I'd been out beyond Aunt Cecily's nurturing walls since Marcus had begun plastering my face on social media.

"Here we are," Langston announced as he parked, and with a deep breath, I braced myself for the torrent of sensations I knew awaited me inside.

The door swung open with a familiar creak, and a wave of sound and warmth rushed forth to greet us. Voices mingled with laughter and the clinking of glasses, forming a tapestry of human connection that I once wove myself into easily. It was like a foreign language I had forgotten how to speak.

"Are you okay?" Langston's handsome face crinkled in concern. I offered him a small, appreciative nod, finding solace in his attentiveness.

"Let's find a seat," I suggested, attempting to steady the fluttering in my stomach as we navigated through the clusters of patrons. I didn't want to sit in the VIP area like last time. That was an invitation for a spotlight. I felt exposed with an irrational fear that a pair of eyes might recognize me among the crowd—not as the artist I was, but as the broken remnant I had become.

"Here's perfect," Langston said, guiding us to a secluded corner table that offered a semblance of privacy. As he pulled out a chair for me, the simple act like a lifeline, grounding me back to the present moment.

"Thank you," I murmured, sliding into the seat with a grace I didn't feel. My hands found each other under the table, fingers intertwining in a silent prayer for strength—or perhaps invisibility.

"You're welcome," he replied, his gaze lingering with a mix of concern and admiration that sent a ripple of unease through me. His gaze trailed over the dress I'd chosen. A glittery fabric that hung loose and low in the front, showing off a peek of cleavage. I crossed my legs, and his eyes drifted down my body in appreciation.

"Tonight's about enjoying the moment," Langston reminded me when he occupied the seat opposite. "Nothing more."

"Enjoying the moment," I echoed internally, allowing the mantra to take root.

The lounge was a cacophony of clinking glasses, laughter, and the soft strumming of a guitar warming up. The dim lights cast shadows that played upon the walls, enveloping the room in an intimate and exposing ambiance.

"Is the lighting too dim? Do you want to sit closer to the stage?" Langston's voice cut through the din, his words wrapped in the silk of his concern.

I shook my head, a small smile tugging at the corners of my lips. "It's perfect," I assured him, though the flutter in my stomach belied my calm exterior. The air was thick with anticipation, every poet, singer, and dreamer in the room awaiting their turn to bare their souls to an audience of kindred spirits.

Langston was wearing dark jeans that hugged his thighs just right, and a simple tee with some anime character I didn't recognize. It was fitted, and it outlined the contours of his chest. His demeanor epitomized sexy casual—effortlessly stylish without trying too hard. It was my turn to admire.

"Can I get you something to drink, Aurora?" His tone had an undercurrent of protectiveness, a silent acknowledgment of the nerves I couldn't quite hide.

"Water, please," I replied, watching as he navigated toward the bar with a fluidity that spoke of confidence. He moved with a sense of purpose, his entire being radiating a protective aura that enveloped me from afar.

I took in the scene before me as he waited for our drinks. On-stage, another hopeful artist adjusted the microphone stand, fingers trembling with the weight of vulnerability. I could sense the collective heartbeat of the room.

"Here you go." Langston's return snapped me back to reality. "And I asked the bartender to keep the ice to a minimum; I know how you hate when it's too cold."

"Thank you," I whispered, ur fingers brushed as I took it.

"Remember, we're here to enjoy. No pressure." Aunt Cecily had suggested I perform tonight. I had a song in my heart, but I declined. But Langston had spent enough time around my Aunt to know that she had selective hearing regarding the word 'no.'

Enjoy, I repeated internally. I was trying, but every eye, every raised cellphone that looked remotely like it might be recording, unnerved me.

I wanted to make music. Not be a public spectacle. Marcus knew this, and that's why he knew the shit he was pulling would mess with me.

When performances began the world around me transformed, and the worries blended into the background. Each artist who took the stage wove their magic, and I became lost in them—one story, one song, one verse at a time. The rawness of their expressions and the courage in their delivery drew me in until I forgot to be afraid.

"Up next, we've got Malcolm with some spoken word!" Aunt Cecily announced. Today, she wore a harem-style jumpsuit full of colors, large gold hoop earrings, and her hair in a high bun. Always stylish.

A moment later, Malcolm's tall and wiry frame took the spotlight.

He stood before us, unassuming yet commanding, as he began to recite his piece. His words were a powerful cascade, each deliberate, striking a chord of truth that resonated through the room's hush. He spoke of struggle, triumph, and streets that nurtured and suffocated dreams.

When Malcolm's final words hung in the air, the thunderous applause followed. The crowd was moved, vibrating with the energy he'd summoned into the space. He bounded off the stage toward our table, cheesing ear-to-ear with the high of his performance.

"Malcolm, that was incredible," I said, my voice threaded with genuine admiration. "You have an amazing gift."

"Thank you, Aurora." His smile was humble, but his eyes danced with the fire of an artist. "I love working at the community center, but poetry—it's my lifeblood. If I could, I'd do this full-time."

He pulled up a chair and sat down.

"Then you should," I encouraged. "Your words—they change the air in a room. That's not just talent; it's power."

"Means a lot, coming from you," he said, acknowledging the mutual respect between artists.

Even amidst the whirling emotions of the evening, I found solace in our conversation, a reminder that real performance art can be lifechanging.

"Speaking of changing lives," Malcolm continued, turning to Langston with a hopeful glint, "you should come down to the center more often, man. Those kids need someone like you as a mentor."

Langston's hand brushed against my knee under the table—a silent reassurance, maybe, or a shared anxiety. "I don't know, Malcolm. I'm an astrophysics professor. Kids look up to athletes, not academics."

"That's not true," I chimed in. "You have so much to offer, Langston. They need role models who show them that their minds can take them places as well as their bodies. Someone who looks like them, who's made it out—it's powerful."

He gave me a thoughtful look, one that said he was weighing my words against his doubts.

"Alright," Langston finally conceded, an impish smile curving his lips, "I'll consider it—but only if you get up there tonight and sing something for us."

My heart skipped. "Me? Sing?" The idea sent a flock of butterflies rampaging through my stomach. I had done it last time--but that was when I was just Cecily's niece from out of town. Now, at least to a few people, I was probably that attention-starved crazy chick trying to ruin an upcoming artist. "I...I can't."

"Come on, Aurora. It's been too long since your voice filled a room," Malcolm encouraged, joining Langston's playful challenge.

"Y'all don't understand. My confidence—it's not what it used to be." The words came out wrapped in layers of self-doubt.

But they wouldn't let it go. Langston mentioned not letting Marcus silence me. I gave him a weary look, which he ignored. Apparently he'd been hanging out with my aunt too long.

The pair even caught Aunt Cecily's eye, pointing at me to indicate I should be announced. Between Langston's gentle nudges, Malcolm's enthusiastic persuasion, and Aunt Cecily's announcement to the room, I stood, legs trembling, as I made my way to the stage. A spotlight followed me, casting a warm glow over my path.

"Can I use the keyboard?" I asked one of the house band members who played between performances.

"Of course," she replied, her encouragement a soft nudge toward the instrument.

As I settled onto the stool, my fingers found their place among the ivory keys. The opening notes to Nina Simone's "Love Me or Leave Me" began to flow slower and more contemplative than the original. Each chord pulsed into the lounge, wrapping around the audience like a tender embrace.

The lyrics spilled from my lips, soulful and yearning, and with each verse, the lounge faded away until it was just me and the music—and Langston. My gaze found him in the crowd, and something within me stirred, a recognition of something deeper than admiration. *Was this what it felt like to teeter on the edge of falling in love?*

I mean, I thought I loved Marcus. But now, looking back, I realize that wasn't love. That was lust? Need? Desperation?

This was different.

As the song unfolded, my voice caressed each word, making the performance an intimate confession of my heart's longing. And though I sang to a room full of listeners, every note and inflection was a secret whispered only to Langston.

When the last note lingered in the air, applause erupted around me, but Langston's expression—rapt, touched—remained etched into my memory.

Langston

My heart was in my throat, an odd sensation for a man more accustomed to the cold logic of astrophysics than the tumultuous world of emotions. But watching Aurora on that stage, something shifted within me. Her voice resonated like gravitational waves bending spacetime—inescapable and elemental.

"Man, she's got pipes," Malcolm whispered beside me, his words barely registering over the thunderous applause that filled the room as Aurora's performance ended.

I nodded, unable to find my voice, which seemed to have taken a hiatus, leaving me stranded in a sea of unspoken admiration. Her eyes lingered on me during the performance, and I felt that it wasn't just the song she delivered; it was a message, an invisible thread weaving between us, pulling taut with every note.

"Did you see that? The way she looked at you? That's love looks, man." Malcolm nudged me, his grin spreading from ear to ear.

"Maybe."

My murmur dissolved in the crowd's swelling applause as Aurora returned to our table. Yet, all I could focus on was the subtle quiver in her hands and her vulnerable smile.

Malcolm stood with arms spread wide—bear hug first, then an exaggerated smack of lips against her cheekbone. She seemed surprised but flashed him a big, warm smile.

"Celestial," I said as she reclaimed her seat next to me.

"Thank you," she said, her eyes meeting mine. "For believing in me."

Her gratitude struck a chord within me, a reminder of my insecurities, of the fear that someone like her might find me lacking. But here, at this moment, it was clear that whatever we were to each other was enough.

"Always," I replied as Malcolm excused himself, leaving us enclosed in a bubble of mutual recognition.

The lounge continued to buzz with activity, but for me, the world had narrowed down to this singular point: Aurora and I sat on the precipice of something new, something terrifyingly beautiful. And as I watched her laugh, the sound more intoxicating than any melody, I realized that this—this moment, this feeling, this woman—was what I had been searching for among the stars.

"Langston," she said, still carrying the remnants of her performance's passion, "thank you for pushing me up there."

"Trust me, it was completely selfish. I needed to hear you sing again," I confessed, the truth slipping out smoother than I'd expected. It was as if I couldn't control myself. My traitorous hand rose unbidden—and there it was: her cheekbone cradled in my palm like Cassiopeia cradles stars. She leaned in, and I felt a familiar dichotomy—cardiac arrest below my collar bones versus reckless heat pooling lower.

If I didn't take a moment away, I'd be dragging her into the bathroom and pulling that damn sexy dress up.

"Would you like another drink?" I asked, gesturing toward the bar.

"Sure," she replied, her gaze lingering on mine before I stood, the residual heat from her palm imprinting through my sleeve propelled me barward.

A thought nagged at the edge of my mind as I waited for the bartender to attend to me. It was more than admiration for Aurora; it was a spiritual tether that seemed to have anchored itself deep within my core. Yet, fear gnawed at me--that I might not be enough despite this connection. An astrophysicist with a penchant for anime and an upbringing from the Southside of Chicago—how could I possibly maintain the interest of a sexy, artistic African American woman whose voice commanded the attention of any room?

"Two bourbons, neat," I ordered, trying to shake off the doubt. The amber liquid seemed to hold the promise of warmth and courage, something I desperately needed.

"Here you go, Professor," the bartender said, sliding the glasses across the polished surface.

I smirked, realizing that I'd been coming here so much recently that they knew me.

"Thanks," I replied, the title oddly constrictive in this setting.

I turned, drinks in hand, the crowd's enthusiastic chatter a backdrop to my racing thoughts. As I approached our table, my heart seized at the sight before me—a large, muscular man leaned aggressively into Aurora's personal space. His body language was all bravado and intimidation, his arm braced against the wall behind her.

"Look, I said I'm not interested," Aurora's voice cut through the din, assertive yet laced with annoyance.

"Come on, baby, don't be like that," the man persisted, his tone patronizing.

My steps quickened as Aurora caught sight of me, her eyes flashing a silent plea for rescue. "I'm here with my boyfriend," she stated vehemently, nodding in my direction. "You should leave me alone."

The man's gaze shifted from Aurora to me, sizing me up with a sneer. "Him?" he scoffed, disbelief etching his features as they settled on my clean-cut appearance. "You expect me to believe a fine thing like you is with this nerd?"

Anger flared within me, but it was quickly doused by a flash of panic at his insinuation. *How dare he question what Aurora saw in me? But then, wasn't I questioning the same thing?*

"Hey," I interjected, setting the drinks down and stepping between Aurora and the intruder. "She asked you to leave. You need to respect that."

The man's dark eyes narrowed, his frame rigid with defiance. The lounge seemed to contract around us for a moment, the sounds of revelry fading into the background. He leaned closer, his breath foul with the stench of alcohol as he whispered menacingly, "Or what?"

His hand moved subtly, his jacket parting to reveal the ominous glint of metal—a concealed weapon. My heart thrummed against my ribcage, every academic accolade meaningless in the face of raw street confrontation. Yet, backing down was not an option when Aurora's safety was at stake.

"Or nothing," I said, meeting his gaze unflinchingly. "Just walk away. There's no need for this to get ugly."

Inside, my mind raced with calculations of risk and trajectories, a far cry from the celestial bodies I was accustomed to studying. But there was one undeniable truth: I would protect Aurora, whatever the cost. And while it was always the last option, I could handle myself fine.

Aurora's eyes locked onto mine as I faced the threat before us. Her gaze was a mix of fear and gratitude, an unspoken plea for this to end peacefully. We caught the attention of a few of the people close enough to hear the interaction. The lounge's noises of clinking glasses and laughter seemed to recede, leaving only the tense standoff at the forefront.

"Man, you don't want to do this," I said, my voice steady despite the adrenaline coursing through me. "We're here for a good time, not to cause trouble."

"Speak for yourself," he sneered, his hand still nonchalantly resting where his weapon was concealed. His disbelief that Aurora would choose someone like me was written all over his face, but it only fueled my resolve.

"Listen," I began again, carefully measuring my words, "she's with me. And we'd appreciate it if you'd respect that and move on."

The man scoffed, sizing me up with blatant disdain. "With you? You think I'm buying that?"

Aurora stepped closer to me, her presence reassuring at my side. "Yes, I'm with him. My *boyfriend*. So please, leave us alone."

The muscular man's lips curled into a sneer, his incredulity hanging between us. But as the seconds ticked by, the tension in his shoulders eased, and he finally took a step back, though his expression remained one of scornful skepticism.

A moment later, another presence was over my shoulder. Malcolm came back and stood right behind me, staring the man down.

"Come on, man," Malcolm interjected, his voice a calm breeze. "You really gonna pull a piece in here over some words? Think about it."

Aurora stood firm beside me, chest rising. "This is pointless," she said, her voice slicing through the heavy music beats in the background. "Let it go."

"Stupid bitch," the man spat out, his words like daggers aimed at Aurora's heart. "Marcus said you were trouble."

The mention of Marcus seemed to make Aurora tense, her eyes widening. Her face mirrored someone taking a sucker punch. The anger searing through me was quickly replaced by an overwhelming need to take her in my arms and comfort her.

"Let's get out of here," I said, my protective arm slipping around Aurora's shoulders.

Outside, the night air embraced us. Aurora trembled against me.

"Are you okay?" I looked down, searching her face for signs of the vibrant woman who had captivated the lounge only moments ago with her sultry voice and passionate performance.

"Marcus has no right... no right to haunt me like this," she murmured, her voice cracking under the weight of memories best left behind.

"Let me take you home," I muttered. If I ever met this Marcus dude, I was gonna give him an ass whooping he wouldn't forget.

Aurora

The silence in my house was thick, cushioning us in its embrace after the tumultuous night. Langston sat across from me, his elbows resting on his knees as he leaned forward, worry marring his handsome features. He held a glass of untouched liquor in his hands. We had left the lounge far behind, but the echo of conflict hummed like a plucked bass string between us.

"Are you warm enough?" Langston's voice broke the stillness, velvety and low. I nodded, tucking my feet under me on the sofa. The room's warmth was comforting, starkly contrasting with the chill that settled in my bones outside the club.

"Thank you... for taking care of me," I murmured, my eyes tracing the lines of worry that furrowed his brow. There was something so inherently protective about him, a sturdiness that belied his gentle demeanor.

"Always, Aurora," he replied with a soft intensity, his gaze locked with mine. "I just wish..." He trailed off, his hand rubbing the back of his neck—a gesture of unease.

"Langston?" I prompted, tilting my head, encouraging him to share what weighed on his mind.

He sighed, his eyes reflecting a storm of emotions. "I wish I could do more to make all this go away. To make you forget Marcus and everything he put you through."

My heart swelled at his words. "You're doing more than you know," I admitted. "Being here with me, listening... it means the world."

"Music is your world, Aurora. Tonight on that stage you were... ethereal." A smile played on his lips, admiration shining through. "And I would fight any battle to see you shine like that."

"Langston," I murmured. "Back there, at the lounge... you were ready to..." I trailed off, unsure how to voice the vivid image of his clenched jaw and resolved stance as he faced that menacing man.

"Fight?" He finished for me, his voice low but not without a hint of steel. "I was, Aurora. It might surprise you, coming from a man who spends his days with his head in the stars."

I nodded, my heart still thrumming erratically from the memory. "It does. I've never seen you like that—so... so willing to be violent. It scared me, Langston."

He sighed, setting his glass aside as if it weighed too much. His dark eyes locked with mine, turbulent as storm clouds. "I didn't mean to frighten you," he confessed. "But there's something you should know about me."

His confession drew me in, and I leaned forward. His presence filled the space, emanating an aura of raw honesty.

"I grew up on the Southside, Aurora. It wasn't easy. Where standing your ground kept breath in your lungs." He paused, the weight of his past settling visibly on his broad shoulders. "I've fought battles before. Some with words, and yes, some with fists. I prefer to always use the former, but saying I've *never* fought would be a lie. I was taught to fight because of where I lived. And I was angry because of where I lived. And I fought because of where I lived. I'm a professor now, yes, but I haven't forgotten where I come from. I am no punk."

"I never thought you were," I said, reaching out to cover his hand.

"Being with you," he continued, his voice dropping to a whisper, "made me feel things I haven't felt in a long time. Feelings of inadequacy that I thought I'd buried deep. I see you—your talent, your beauty—and I wonder if I'm enough. And his words cut, because it's like he saw my fear. And it made me angry."

"Langston..." I started, but he lifted a finger to halt my reply.

"Let me finish, please. Tonight, when that man threatened you, all those insecurities roared back to life. But I couldn't just stand by. Not when it comes to you." His eyes held mine, unwavering. "I apologize if my actions upset you. That's the last thing I want."

"Thank you for telling me this," I whispered, squeezing his hand. His vulnerability shone through, as clear and striking as the melodies I sang. It was then I realized the depth of his feelings, the battle he fought within himself—a fight I recognized all too well.

"Langston," I began again, stronger this time, "you are enough. More than enough. And I need you to know that." My voice wavered with emotion, echoing against the quiet walls, reverberating through us both.

And in the dim light of my home, with the night winding down around us, I saw Langston—the man of constellations and dreams, the protector, the seeker of knowledge—as someone who also needed to be understood and accepted, just as much as I did.

"Langston," I murmured, leaning in so my breath feathered across his neck, "I know what it's like to feel... less. Marcus had this way of praising me, yet always leaving a 'but' hanging in the air. Like a note held too long, souring the melody."

He pulled back enough to look at me, the shadows playing upon his face. "Aurora, you have this power in you—when you perform, it's undeniable." His voice was a velvet whisper, sincerity threading through each word. "Tonight, when you sang, you weren't just good enough, you were transcendent."

A shiver ran through me, not from cold but from the realization that bloomed within me—a delicate, burgeoning hope. The way he looked at me stripped away every lie Marcus' words had etched into my skin.

"Transcendent?" My throat tightened around the word I'd only dreamed of owning. "You think so?"

"Absolutely."

My heart hammered against my ribs—a staccato rhythm syncopating with newfound hope. *Could I? Could I allow myself to fall for this man who looks at me as if I composed the stars?*

"Langston," I said, straddling his lap, my hands framing his face. "You don't ever have to feel like you're not enough. Not for me, not for anyone." The intensity in my gaze matched the conviction in my voice.

My heart hammered against my ribs—a staccato rhythm syncopating with newfound hope. "You really mean that?" He chuckled lightly, a sound that bubbled up from somewhere deep and genuine. "Especially after you declared me your boyfriend to scare off that guy."

"Did I now?" A playful lilt colored my words, even as my pulse thrummed with the gravity of what we were admitting to each other. "Well, I wasn't exactly fibbing."

His laughter faded into a look of awe, as if he were seeing me for the first time. "Aurora, there's nothing I want more than to be that man for you-"

My breath caught as Langston's lips met mine, a touch tender yet filled with an unspoken promise.

"Langston," I whispered against his mouth.

He responded, not with words, but by deepening his kiss, his hands finding the small of my back to pull me closer.

Could this be real? Am I ready to trust this, trust us?

As usual, it was as if Langston heard the whispers of my soul. "You're everything," he said, his voice husky. "Don't ever question it."

A spark lit a fire in my belly, and I pressed down, his mound hardened underneath me. My fingers trailed up his low fade and down his delicious jawline coated in soft bristles.

"Show me," I urged, my eyes locked on his. "Show me I'm enough for you."

With a groan that rumbled through his chest, Langston lifted and carried me towards the bedroom.

He put me on the bed and then simply looked down at me.

This is what it means to be seen.

Langston's gaze traced the contours of my face, down the length of my neck, and across the curves Marcus had once claimed were never quite perfect.

But in Langston's eyes, I saw no such criticisms—only admiration, only want.

"Beautiful," he breathed out, his hand cupping my cheek before trailing downwards, mapping the journey his eyes had taken moments ago.

"Langston..." My voice trembled, a mixture of nerves and need making my limbs quake.

"His fingers skimmed my zipper before peeling fabric from skin; his own pants and underwear pooled at his feet. When he reached to take the shirt off, I placed a gentle hand to stop him.

"I like it." I admired how the material pulled across his chest. He smirked, grabbed me roughly, and flipped me over. Two strong hands pulled my ass in the air as he kneeled on the bed behind me.

A moment later, heat bloomed where his mouth branded flesh I'd deemed unremarkable until now. He was lightly dragging his wet tongue across my rear.

"What... what are you doing-?"

"Tracing our favorite constellation on your ass." He kissed a spot on my left cheek. A thumb entered between my crack. He lightly pushed the pad right on the hole. He didn't enter, but unexpected pressure sent a shiver up my spine.

He dragged his tongue in an arch across my lower back and planted a kiss on my right cheek. He pushed with this thumb harder.

"Ohh..."

Then I felt the graze of those hairs teasing the line. He moved his thumb, both hands gripped a cheek, then he slowly separated them. I wanted to see him and tried to turn to look at him. A wicked grin, followed by a wink, was all I got before he pushed me back in position.

Then there was his mouth. The soft hair grazed parts of my ass never touched by a man, and his tongue slid from the dip of my back to right before the hole.

"His graveled growl against my ear raised gooseflesh—more plea than demand: "Want this?"

"Yes," was all I could manage to whimper. I heard movement as he sheathed himself. A finger, then two, went into my pussy.

"Good and fuckin' ready." He entered quick and rough, and I'd be fucked if I didn't see stars. His hips slammed against my ass. A moment later, his thumb was back at the hole, this time pushing harder. As he pumped into me, I heard him say my name.

The tip of the thumb slipped in. I'd never had that before, but it felt amazing.

"God, you're like..." Langston's words dissolved into a moan as he began to pummel me harder from behind.

"Tell me," I insisted, needing to hear his pleasure verbalized, to understand the depth of his desire.

"Like heaven," he managed to say, between strokes.

And as we moved together, a chorus of sighs and whispers filled the air. It was like music.

"Langston!" I yelled as a shock wave hit me, sending shutter after shutter of pleasure through me. It must have triggered him because a moment later, he was joining me. He stopped moving and gripped my ass cheeks so hard I knew there would be marks.

But I didn't care. As he unloaded himself, the pressure built inside me and another orgasm rippled through me. He shuttered, then collapsed on me, and immediately rolled his weight off. The second his penis left me, I felt empty.

"Fucking shit, Aurora," was all he muttered, that beautiful chest of his rising and falling.

I couldn't even speak. Instead, I stretched out right next to him, every nerve still humming like a tuning fork struck true.

Chapter 7

Aurora

As I sat alone in the living room of the little apartment I borrowed from my Aunt, I couldn't help but reminisce about the journey that had brought me here. Langston had gone to work and left me with my thoughts. He'd all but moved in since I almost had a breakdown. During the few times he wasn't there to comfort me, my mind drifted.

Coming from a family of talented visual artists, I had always been the odd one out as the first performance artist among them. I used to feel so insecure about my abilities that I could never measure up to the masterpieces my family created with their hands. But eventually, with their encouragement and the support of my music instructors, I began to believe in my talent. Before my mother died all she did was tell me how talented I was.

I met Marcus a bit after she'd died, and he filled the void left by her quickly. Our shared passion for music drew us together, and it wasn't long before I fell under his spell. Even then, I could see hints of jealousy lurking beneath his charming exterior, but I ignored them. In hindsight, I wish I had paid more attention to those warning signs.

Our relationship began as a friendship, but it didn't take long for Marcus and I to become lovers. He was undeniably sexy and dynamic, with a magnetic personality that drew me in. But beneath his alluring facade, he harbored a darker side that would slowly chip away at my self-esteem and confidence.

Marcus had this insidious way of making me doubt my talent.

It's a good song, but I don't know, he'd say about a song I wrote. *Something is missing.* Then he'd change literally one word and call himself my co-writer.

Or, *You sound 'aight, but it ain't really for a voice like yours.*

My words became his words—melodies ripped raw from my throat repackaged as his genius rent-free. And let him because he asked so sweet, and was so good at faking love, and could twist things so I thought that anyone hearing the song, even if it wasn't sung by me, was a victory.

He loved pointing out how my voice was deeper than most girls. My Aunt said it was bass, and soulful. Marcus said it was *mannish*. So, I was happy with all the love that poured through social media for the original music he posted. I was foolish enough to think we were sharing the applause.

We'd always perform songs a few times before Marcus recorded them. Kind of like rehearsals. At first, when Tony "discovered" us singing the original music at a lounge in our college town, it was exciting. We went to meetings with record labels, were introduced as two up-and-coming artists. Then Tony started introducing me as one of the songwriters. Then, I was introduced as the band leader. Then one of the band.

Soon, I wasn't even invited to the meetings.

Baby, it's cool. This is us. It don't matter who go to the meetings... it don't matter whose name is on the contract... it don't matter whose name is in the front. We better together... You're better with me.

And I believed that shit. He had me thinking his breath gave mine oxygen—that without him pumping life into me daily, I was just airless space. As time passed, I started to believe him more and more, and my music started to die.

But I thought he loved me. I thought his success was our success.

It wasn't until later in our relationship that I began to pick up hints and clues that Marcus was cheating on me. Side eyes from people when I entered a room on his arm. Men and women that were just a bit too bold with him in my presence. Slight little comments about me being a fool.

Whenever I confronted him about it, he would call me crazy and obsessive, insisting that he'd never betray me. But deep down, I knew something was off.

I shouldn't have been surprised when I found him that day. I was supposed to run the band through a music rehearsal for an out-of-town show we were planning, but I forgot something and ran back to the hotel room to grab it. I could hear the man through the door.

Fuck, man. That's that shit. Just like that. It was as if I could hear that voice right now.

But it wasn't Marcus' voice. The hairs on my neck stood up now just thinking about it. When I opened the door, it was like a fucking ton of bricks hit me in the chest.

There they were--Marcus and Tony butt-ass naked in the middle of the bed Marcus had fucked me in the night before.

I remember screaming, yelling, throwing shit. But somehow, I remember it being twisted to be my fault. I wasn't supposed to be there. He never made me any promises. It wasn't his fault if I thought I was exclusive. It wasn't cheating really because he wasn't with another woman.

Marcus twisted the situation and made it seem as though his cheating was my fault—that I wasn't enough to satisfy him. I remember that look on that bastard Tony's face--that he could do what I couldn't. It was yet another cruel blow to my already fragile self-worth.

And no one would believe me. Marcus, one of the biggest upcoming sex symbols, was cheating with another man. And both of them had been together under my nose for months before I realized.

I sounded crazy to the band when I told them. Even Tony's wife and business partner, Maria, didn't back me even though she seemed like she believed me. Thinking back, the look on some of their faces registered they thought it was possible.

But whose side would anyone take? After all, I was a bitter woman who wasn't sure of her self-worth. He was a successful musician and songwriter. A sex symbol.

Of course, no one believed me. And those who might kept their mouths shut.

Now I realized how far I had come from those dark days with Marcus. I hadn't expected to meet anyone like Langston.

He supported me. He believed in me. He uplifted me.

I wasn't used to it. For the first time since Marcus had kicked me out of the apartment, the band, and his life, I felt like my true self. My music was coming back to me.

It was a slow and painful process, rebuilding myself after losing not only my partner but also my music—my very soul. Marcus had taken so much from me, denying that I was the true author of many songs that propelled him to fame. My career had been left in tatters, and at times, I couldn't help but think it was partially my fault.

Those glances I caught between them. The times I caught them whispering or touching. I should have recognized the signs of Marcus and Tony's relationship. I mean, Tony wasn't the only man I found Marcus' relationship with to be, well, questionable. I had the same vibe with him around some men as I did with him around some women. Marcus had always been open with everyone--men, women, didn't matter. He enjoyed being a sex symbol. That wasn't my issue. It was that he steadily told me it was all for show, he would never follow through. He was an artist, and he was just expressing himself.

Bullshit. He was a cheater. It didn't matter if it was a man or a woman. I had been so blinded by love and my insecurities that I missed it all.

But to be honest, to have him turn to a man and literally say *Aurora, you just wasn't enough woman for me* hurt like hell.

Yet, here I was now, with Langston—a man who saw the real me, loved me for who I was, and encouraged me to embrace my talent. I could feel the warmth of his presence even when he wasn't physically near me. His steady love reminds me how unbroken parts still bloom.

I hadn't told anyone that I began to write again; the melodies and lyrics flowing through me like they once did before Marcus had torn them away.

The first time Langston and I made love, it was tender and passionate in a way I had never experienced before. It was as if our souls connected deeper, beyond the physical act of intimacy. With Marcus, it had always been about power and control. It fed his ego more than my hunger—all heat no heart.

As I lay in Langston's arms later that night, after a particularly intense session, I couldn't help but compare my experiences with him to those I'd had with Marcus. The more I thought about it, the clearer it became that what I shared with Langston was genuine, while everything with Marcus had been a carefully constructed illusion.

"Hey," Langston whispered, brushing a stray curl from my forehead. "You okay?"

I smiled, my heart swelling with emotion for this man who had shown me that true passion and connection came from being open and honest with one another. "Yeah, I'm more than okay."

"Good," he murmured, pulling me closer and kissing the top of my head.

"Langston," I whispered, realizing now was the perfect time to share my surprise with him. "There's something I want to tell you."

"Anything, baby," he replied, his voice warm and inviting.

"Remember when I told you I hadn't sung or written any of my music since everything happened?" I asked hesitantly.

"Of course," he said, concern etched into his features.

"Well, that's not entirely true. Since I've been with you, I've started writing again. And, um... I have a surprise for you at Open Mic Night."

"Really?" Langston's face lit up, and I could see the excitement dancing in his eyes. "What kind of surprise?"

"You'll have to wait and see," I teased, my excitement growing as I imagined Langston's reaction to my performance.

"Alright, I can't wait," he said, his grin infectious. "I know it will be amazing, like you."

Langston

The venue hummed with bodies pressed toward the stage, waiting for the next performer. The Open Mic Night had become a local favorite. I scanned the crowd, my throat tightened like I'd swallowed starlight as I thought about Aurora's surprise.

"Next up, we have a very special performer," Aunt Cecily announced. Tonight, the woman was rocking a skin-tight yellow dress with purple squiggly lines and a split straight up to her thigh. All the men were gawking, and Aurora kept quipping about how fine the women in her family aged. I only had eyes for Aurora, but I wouldn't argue with the truth. "Please give a warm welcome to Aurora!"

The applause was thunderous as Aurora confidently walked onto the stage, her skin gleamed like burnished amber under the spotlight. Her eyes found mine in the crowd, and she gave me a nervous but excited smile. There was electricity between us, even from a distance.

"Good evening, everyone," she began, her voice strong and clear. "I've been up here a few times, but tonight is different. Tonight, I'd like to sing an original song that I wrote, inspired by someone very dear to my heart. This is for you, Langston."

My pulse stuttered against my collar as her fingers danced over her guitar strings, strumming the introduction of her love song. The melody was enchanting, drawing me in with every note. Her voice was filled with raw emotion as she sang, each word resonating deep within me.

In your eyes, I see constellations, a galaxy so bright,
Each glance--a supernova--igniting endless light,

With every kiss, we travel, like comets in the skies,

Guided by love's gravity, where true love never dies.

A wave of emotion passed over me. Aurora kept singing, her eyes locked on mine.

Oh, you're my North Star, my guiding light,

In your love, I find my way, every single night,

Through the galaxies of your soul, we take flight,

In this cosmic love story, our hearts unite.

Damn, this woman was singing to my soul. Each verse painted a picture of our connection, capturing the wildfire heat of us. She'd cracked open my chest and strummed my ribs like guitar strings.

As she finished the song, the room erupted in applause. I couldn't help but marvel at how this woman had somehow captured all my feelings and put it to music. It was breathtaking to witness.

"Thank you," she whispered into the microphone, her eyes locked on mine. "Thank you for showing me what love can be."

Between waves of Egyptian Musk, vanilla perfume, and hoarse cheers, I caught a flash of freckled cheeks. The woman swung her recording camera from the stage to track Aurora as she made her way toward me, mouth curled like she'd bitten into something sour.

"Langston!" Aurora called, snapping me out of my thoughts as she approached me.

"Baby, that was incredible," I told her, wrapping my arms around her. "Your song... it was beautiful. You're beautiful."

"Thank you," she replied, her eyes shining with happiness. "I couldn't have done it without you."

"Who, me?" I teased, smiling down at her. "All I did was show you a few constellations. The rest is all you."

As we shared a passionate kiss, I noticed the woman with the freckles had pivoted her camera and was recording our private moment, her smug expression unchanged. However, before I could break away from Aurora to confront her, the woman disappeared into the crowd. Aurora looked at me confused, but I just tightened my arms around her and gave into a passionate kiss while hoping that icy spider-crawl down my spine wasn't a warning.

Chapter 8

Aurora

The morning sun spilt its honeyed light across the kitchen counter, casting a warm glow on the bowl of fresh fruit that sat in the center. I stood there, lost in the rhythmic dance of slicing strawberries, the rich reds and greens mingling with the golden sunlight. The sizzle of eggs in the pan is my culinary symphony, accompanied by the comforting aroma of coffee brewing in the background. Langston was still sprawled out in bed, and I wanted to make him something before he went to work.

I smiled to myself, feeling almost domestic. I was a lot of things, but housewife material wasn't one. However, pretending for a little while was fun.

My phone buzzed against the wooden table. I wipe my hands on the apron tied around my waist before reaching for it. The screen lights up with a name I haven't seen since the days when music was a shared dream, not a battleground – Joanne, a saxophonist whose laughter could brighten even the dreariest of rehearsals. I used to like that chick.

"Hey, Aurora, you need to see this," her message reads, followed by a link. "Marcus is losing it."

A knot tightens in my stomach. I tap the link. The video loads, and there I am, eyes closed, lost in the melody as I strum the guitar. My soul seems to seep through the strings, pouring out into the room of the open mic night from a few days ago... but that now seems like a lifetime ago.

"Your voice...it's still so haunting," Joanne texts again, her words pulling me back from the memory.

"Thanks, Joanne. It was something small, nothing big," I reply, trying to keep the tremble from my fingertips as they tap against the screen.

"Small? That song is amazing! And that hottie you were singing to! Girl, Marcus is in your shadow now. Everyone's talking about it."

I let out a soft sigh, torn between the flicker of pride warring with fresh anxiety at Marcus' name. His presence clings like smoke - sweet incense turned choking smog.

"Is he okay?" I type, my concern genuine despite everything.

"Hard to say. But Aurora, people are seeing you now. Just you."

I set the phone down, my hand trembling, as conflicting emotions wage war within me. Part of me wants to reach and contact him, to make sure he was alright. How sick is that? Marcus was an ass. But he did have some talent. And at one point, I did love him.

"Focus." My knife hits the cutting board harder than intended as I turn back to the stove to rescue the eggs that threaten to overcook. "This is your new beginning, not another verse in the same old song."

The sharp hiss from the pan anchors me. I sprinkled some salt and this chili lime seasoning I snagged from my aunt. My phone buzzes again. It's another message from my former bandmate.

"Industry folks are whispering that Marcus hasn't been the same since you left. You were always the true talent behind him, Aurora. This performance proves it."

It was followed by another link to a video.

The words seep into me, a mixture of sweet validation and a sharp pang of sorrow for what was once shared between Marcus and me. I inhale deeply, trying to steady the flutter in my chest.

"Thank you," I reply, my thumbs hovering over the keys as I add, "I want to make music, that's all."

With a flick of my wrist, I flip the eggs onto a plate and sit at the kitchen table. Taking a deep breath, I opened the video streaming platform on my laptop and pasted the link.

The page loads, and there it is—the performance from a few nights ago. The whole performance, and even my interaction with Langston after. My heart races as I see the view count—thousands. Scrolling down, I read the comments, a chorus of strangers singing praises I've longed to hear yet feared to believe.

"Her voice is like velvet—so rich and smooth!"

"Who knew Marcus' ex had this kind of talent? He must be kicking himself now!"

"Wait, she the chick that used to play with Marcus James? No wonder his latest tracks lack soul now!"

Each word is a note in a symphony of affirmation, dissonance creating harmony, crafting a song of my own making. A small smile creeps up my face, unbidden but not unwelcome. For so long, my artistry lived in the shadow of Marcus—my muse, my tormentor, my first real love. But here, in these comments, I find an echo of my deepest desire: to be seen for who I am, not just as the girl who stood beside him.

"Is it really happening?" I murmur to myself. The anxiety gripped me earlier loosens its hold, replaced by a cautious optimism. Perhaps the tides are turning, and with them, my fortunes.

My fingers, still trembling with the residue of excitement and anxiety, hover over the screen. I've closed the tab with all the praise, but now there's this gnawing need to know more. What else is out there? What are they saying?

Curiosity killed the cat, Aunt Cecily always warned in her honeyed drawl, but I can't help it. I type my name into the search bar, heart-thumping a bass line against my ribcage. The results flood in—a cascade of headlines and links—but one catches my eye immediately—a gossip blog.

"Exclusive Interview: Food Delivery Girl Spills on Aurora's New Love!" The title flashes like a neon sign, luring me in. I click, and the page loads, revealing an embedded video. It's her—the woman who delivered our items last week. My mouth goes dry as she speaks eagerly into the microphone, a hint of malice beneath her excitement.

"Delivered right to their door," she says with a sly smile. "They were so cute together, totally wrapped up in each other. Madly in love. You can tell they've been an item for ages."

'Madly in love', while there's truth there, it feels invasive, twisted coming from this stranger. I didn't even know this chick. This woman, this stranger, had come to my house. Then she filmed our private exchange...auctioned our vulnerability.

The room tilts, and my breath grows shallow. This wasn't supposed to happen. We were careful, Langston and I. All I needed was the tide to turn, and I'd become the hoe that jumped from one guy to the next.

I was about to pass out as I began breathing short, gasping breaths. I could think his name, but couldn't say it. But he's already here, his lips pulled into a frown.

"Hey, hey, what's wrong?" Langston's warm arms wrapping around me. "Talk to me, Aurora."

"Look." I nod toward the screen, and he leans in, the furrow deepening between his brows as he reads. "She filmed us at the open mic too," I whisper, the reality of it hitting me like violin strings snapping mid-crescendo. "That night was for us. I mean I know people would be there. But to come to a little local open mic to get video and send it to the tabloids-"

"I remember her." Langston's voice is calm but tight. "She was angling that phone pretty conspicuously. Must've sold it all for a quick buck."

"Everything's unraveling," I breathe, my heart beats frantically.

"No, no, look at me." Langston's hands cup my face, turning me to him, his deep brown eyes steady. "We've got this. You've got this. They see you, Aurora. They really see you."

His words are a balm, but the panic lingers—a stubborn stain refusing to be washed away. Can something that feels so much like exposure also be my revelation?

"Come on, let's get some air," he suggests, guiding me towards the door. I refuse to move my feet. Going outside was the last thing I wanted. I bury my face in his chest. Before he can object, I'm pulling his lips toward mine. I needed to feel him.

He pulls me in closer but mumbles, "You burning something."

I turn around, quickly snapped the pilot light under the blackened eggs off, and then turned back to show Langston how much his calming soul meant to me.

It wasn't until after I had rode my release out that I wanted to talk. As I lay in the bed, wrapped in his warm embrace, I whispered, "Langston, I'm scared."

"Understandable," he acknowledges, holding me tighter. "But maybe this is a chance for you to shine alone."

"Without Marcus," I murmur, the words foreign on my tongue.

"Exactly." His voice is firm but soothing. "People are recognizing your talent, Aurora. They're hearing you, not him. Isn't that what you always wanted?"

I nod, uncertainty warring with a budding sense of hope inside me. Langston is right; there's something invigorating about being acknowledged for my music—my soul's truest expression—without it being overshadowed by Marcus's presence.

The buzzing of our phones pulls us back inside. Messages and notifications cascade like a relentless waterfall. Friends express their shock, their excitement, and their support. That video was making its rounds.

"Look at this," Langston chuckles, showing me a text from a colleague that reads, 'Guess you're dating a star now. Don't forget us little people.'

A smile tugs at the corners of my lips despite everything. "You okay?" I ask, gesturing to his phone.

"Apparently, I'm 'Aurora's mystery man.'" He rolls his eyes, but the amusement is clear. "I've never been a title in someone else's narrative before."

"Welcome to the club," I tease, the warmth in my chest growing as I watch him laugh. It's deep, beautiful, contagious sound, one that eases the tightness in my shoulders.

"Whatever happens next," Langston says, his thumb tracing circles on the back of my hand, "we'll figure it out together."

"Thank you," I whisper, leaning into him. My heart still races, but it's no longer solely from fear. There's also gratitude—for his steadfast presence, the unexpected clarity brought on by chaos, and the art that refuses to be silenced within me.

"Always," he replies, his voice a promise wrapped in the melody only we could compose from discordant notes.

Langston

The hum of anticipation vibrated through the lecture hall as students shuffle in, clutching books and whispering. I turned my back to them to answer a call from Malcolm.

"Hey," Malcolm teased as soon as I picked up, "'Celestial Sexy Scientist.' That moniker might stick around longer than any celestial body you teach us about."

I can't help but laugh at the absurdity while tapping keys. He was using one of the names social media had given me. "Man, if only my research garnered this kind of public attention." My eyes scan today's lecture notes.

"Love has a way of outshining everything else," Malcolm quips.

"Is that so?" I reply, amused. "And here I thought black holes were the ultimate cosmic spotlight stealers."

"Only until Aurora came along," he says, and we both chuckle, our laughter mingling with the growing buzz of the room.

"Seriously though, Lang," his tone softens, "It's wild how things are unfolding. You two... it's like watching a star being born. It's a lot for a dude like you."

"More like a supernova some days," I confess, the weight of the situation pressing down on me even in jest. "But it's true—she's incandescent. People are finally seeing her for the talent she is. I just happen to be standing next to her. "

"About time. But what about you? You good suddenly being thrust into the limelight? When you get awards, they can hardly talk you into making an acceptance speech."

"Let's say it's an adjustment," I answer, my gaze drifting over the sea of faces gathering for the lecture. Some are familiar, regulars in the journey through astrophysics. Others, drawn by curiosity or something else, are new.

"An adjustment," Malcolm muses. "Well, make sure you don't lose sight of your own stars, my friend. Aurora is doing her thing, but you big things too in your circle, man. You were before her, and you'll always be, man."

"Thanks."

We chat for a few minutes before I end the call to focus on my notes for the day.

"Good morning, everyone," I begin, my voice steady as the class quiets. "Today, we'll explore the lifecycle of stars. And trust me, it's more dramatic than any tabloid headline."

As I delve into these celestial giants' birth, life, and death, I draw parallels in my mind. Stars, like us, go through transformative processes, often emerging from their trials more radiant than before.

"Professor Wilkerson?" a voice interrupts my train of thought during a brief pause.

"Yes?"

"Sorry to veer off-topic, but everyone's talking about that video. How you doing with all the attention?"

I pause, considering my words. My gaze searched the darkened seating area, but I couldn't make out any faces. "It's unexpected, certainly," I admit. "But if it sheds light on someone's true brilliance, then perhaps it's not altogether unwelcome."

Nods and murmurs ripple through the crowd, and I refocus on the lesson, leaving the complexities of personal orbits for another time and space.

The lecture flows smoothly from there, the stars and their cosmic dances holding court. As I wrap up the class with a discussion on supernovas—the spectacular death that leads to new life—I can't help but draw a metaphorical line to my life beyond the streets that once confined me.

"Professor Wilkerson?" Jamal's voice cuts into my reverie as the students begin to disperse.

"Jamal, what's up?" I ask, noting his eager stance. His trademark glasses are on top of his head.

"I've come across this thing that might keep me in school," he says, an edge of hope in his voice. "It's a fellowship to design and run a science outreach program. If you could recommend me..."

"Say no more, Jamal. Of course, I'll help." I mean it. The kid has potential that shouldn't be wasted. "Leave your proposal with me. I'll go through it tonight."

"Thanks, man." He grins, visibly relieved. "Hope all this" —he gestures vaguely at the air around us— "won't keep you too busy to remember us little people."

"Too busy?"

He chuckles, motioning toward the room where a few people still stood. "Your new fans. You're a hit, Professor Sexy Scientist."

I glance around. Indeed, the hall has a few more students than normal lingering, most notably a group of young women whispering and stealing glances in my direction. One of them catches my eye, a bold smirk on her face.

"We're just auditing"—she paused dramatically—"the Celestial Sexy Scientist's class." Her friends giggling beside her.

A flush of heat creeps up my neck. I'm unaccustomed to this kind of attention. I got the ladies' attention, especially on campus, but this was different. It feels... alien. A part of me wants to retreat to the safety of equations and theories, away from these knowing looks. But another part recognizes the potential impact—this could be a chance to inspire more minds, even if they initially came for the wrong reasons. And the truth is, if I chose to pursue and support Aurora, people would recognize me for that.

"Enjoy the audit," I reply with a wry smile, returning to gather my papers. My mind is already drifting to Aurora, wondering how she's handling her own burst of stardom.

I know that I was lucky not to get a ticket the way I sped across town to Aurora's place. All I wanted was to be back with her, to make sure she was in as high spirits as I left her.

The wind sliced through me as I hurried across the street, coat collar yanked high against both weather and dread. I looked up to the front of the main brick house that Aunt Cecily occupied. There was a large, shiny SUV parked outside. Not entirely unusual. But what was abnormal was the large, menacing man with arms folded who stood outside the separate entrance to Aurora's spot. As I approached, I felt his glare, as cold as the wind that slapped me across the face.

"What's good?" I asked, stopping a few paces in front of him. He responded by looking me up and down, followed by a grunt.

I gave a small grimace and attempted to walk around him.

"Nah," he said, shifting to prevent me from passing.

I stared at him for a minute. "Why you in front of my girl's spot?"

"*Your* girl?" he mocked.

"Yeah, *my* girl." The heat of anger rose. "You better move your overgrown ass."

"For real?" The man puffed up his chest to look bigger--just like an ape. His voice rose an octave. "You gon' move me, professor?"

My eyes narrowed, realizing he knew who I was. "If I have to."

Right before I could decide if my next move was words or fists, the door to Aurora's opened, she stood there, looking surprised and embarrassed. I looked behind her to see the flesh and blood-version of the bastard that had flooded social media. And he looked like just as much of a punchable ass in person. His smug smile and whitened teeth glowed incongruously under Aurora's fluorescent kitchen lights—the same lights where I'd kissed strawberry syrup from her collarbone last Tuesday.

"What's up, professor?" he asked with a comfortable smirk on his face.

Aurora

"Sweetheart, you can't let the past smother your future," Aunt Cecily's voice was like a lullaby, wrapping me in its comfort. We're sitting at my kitchen table, sipping on chamomile tea—the scent of the brew sweet and tranquil. After spending time intertwined with

Langston, I had bundled up to run to the main house for tea with one of my favorite people.

"Your performance was sublime, Aurora. And everyone's starting to notice. Marcus... well, let's just say his solo act isn't quite hitting the same notes without you." She smiles warmly, her eyes twinkling with mischief and pride.

I lean back in the chair, cradling the cup between my palms, allowing its warmth to seep into my skin. "It's hard to believe that people are finally seeing things. For so long, I thought maybe he was right about me..." My voice trails off, and I take a sip of tea to fill the silence.

"Ridiculous!" Aunt Cecily exclaims, her silver bracelets jangling as she dismisses my doubts with a wave. Even at home, she wore the most beautiful things. Today was a beautiful blue kaftan dress accented with silver accessories. "You were always the heart of the music, Aurora. He was just riding on your coattails. Now, it seems, he's stumbled without them."

The steam from the tea rises in gentle swirls, and for a moment, I get lost in its dance. Could it be true? Is the tide of public opinion finally turning in my favor? The thought is both exhilarating and terrifying. I've been hidden in the shadows for so long that the idea of stepping into the spotlight on my own merits sends a shiver down my spine.

"Maybe things are changing," I murmur, more to myself than to Aunt Cecily.

"You have a gift," Aunt Cecily says, reaching across the table to squeeze my hand. "And no one, especially not Marcus, can take that away from you."

I meet her gaze, and something within me shifts—a small ember of belief fanned into a flame. "Thank you, Aunt Cecily. I needed to hear that, really."

"Anytime, my dear. Just remember who you are and where you come from. Your roots are strong and will support you as you grow."

As we continue talking, the outside world fades away, leaving only the sound of our voices mingling with the clink of teacups and the quiet hum of the city beyond the walls.

A sudden, forceful knocking reverberates through the cozy kitchen, startling both of us. Aunt Cecily's eyebrows knit together as she moves towards the door, her movements tinged with an unspoken warning. No one from the neighborhood bothered Aunt Cecily. She's a staple. However, it was still the hood.

With a cautious hand, Aunt Cecily opens the door. The silhouette in the entryway leaves no room for doubt—it's him. Marcus stands there, an ostentatious bouquet of flowers clutched in his hand like a gaudy peace offering. His attire is a carefully curated mix of high fashion and street style—a tailored jacket draping over his broad shoulders, designer jeans hugging his athletic frame, and his feet adorned in shoes worth more than most people's rent.

The jewelry adorning his fingers, wrists, and neck glints in the sunlight, each piece screaming of excess and vanity. But it's not just his appearance that fills the space; it's also the unapologetic arrogance seeping every pore. His smile is all teeth, too wide and rehearsed as if he's selling a version of himself even he doesn't believe in.

"Good morning, ladies," Marcus greets us, his voice smooth like honey but with an underlying note of smugness that makes my skin crawl.

"Marcus," Aunt Cecily responds coolly, her displeasure evident in her clipped tone. "To what do we owe the... unexpected pleasure?"

"Can't a man visit his muse without an agenda?" He tries to charm, stepping into the space as if he owns it, but Aunt Cecily blocks his path with a subtle shift of her stance.

"Your muse?" Her skepticism is almost tangible. "That's a curious way to describe someone you've taken from."

Marcus turns his attention towards me. I shrink back, suddenly exposed and vulnerable under his scrutiny. The progress I thought I'd made in believing in myself evaporates in his presence. I'm that uncertain girl again, who doubted every note she sang and chord she played.

"Can we talk, Aurora?" Marcus says, his eyes locking onto mine. There's a plea there, or at least a facsimile of one.

"Whatever you have to say to Aurora can be said with me present," Aunt Cecily interjects, her protective nature flaring like a shield before me. She crossed her arms.

"Listen, I just—" Marcus starts, but Aunt Cecily isn't having any of it.

"No, you listen," she bites back. "This young woman has been through enough, and if you think for one second—"

"Please," I whisper. "It's okay, Aunt Cecily."

Is it okay? My thoughts are a whirlwind of confusion and fear. Can I handle facing him, or will I crumble under the weight of our shared past?

Marcus's gaze softens fractionally, but I recognize the calculation behind it. He understands the power he holds—or used to hold—and he's ready to wield it once more.

"Let's go somewhere private," he suggests, holding his hand as if expecting me to take it.

"Fine," I concede, though every instinct screams for me to run. "But not far."

Aunt Cecily's eyes narrow, glinting with anger and concern. "Aurora, you don't have to do this," she says, her voice low and urgent.

"I need to," I tell her, though my heart races with trepidation. "I'll be next door. If I don't return in a few minutes, come get me."

"Five minutes," Aunt Cecily warns Marcus with a pointed finger. "And not a second more. Or I swear the flowers will be for your grave."

Marcus nods, though his arrogance doesn't fully leave his stance. He turns, beckoning me to follow him into the brisk air.

We walk silently to my apartment next door, the distance feeling like miles rather than meters. His guard, a towering silhouette of muscle and watchfulness, stands by the entrance but doesn't follow us inside.

I notice a few noisy neighbors looking at us. While my presence had gone mostly unnoted, Marcus had people's attention. That's just how he was. He got stares everywhere he went.

"How did you find me?" I ask once we're alone, my voice steady despite the storm of emotions.

"The video," he replies smoothly, almost too easily. "It's everywhere, Aurora. You look... you look amazing in it."

His compliment hangs in the air, mingling with the faint smell of my jasmine-scented candles. It feels invasive, like a fragrance that doesn't belong.

"Marcus, what do you want?" I press, needing to know his intentions.

He sighs. It sounds rehearsed for effect. "I was wrong," he starts, pacing slowly before me. "I let things spiral out of control between us. I should've supported you, not competed with you."

For a moment, the smoothness in his voice is disarming, and memories flicker through my mind—us laughing together, writing music, dreaming of stages and spotlights. But those moments are stained, tainted by darker recollections of harsh words and cold silences.

"Remember *our* dream?" he continues, turning to face me with earnest eyes that plead for understanding. "To make music, give the world something beautiful?"

The dream feels distant now, a remnant of a person I no longer am—or perhaps never truly was.

"Things are different now, Marcus," I reply, wrapping my arms around myself as if to hold the present reality close. "I'm different."

"Are you?" he challenges. "Or are you still that girl with fire in her soul and a song in her heart? The girl I fell in love with?"

His words wrap around me like a gentle but suffocating vine, creeping with the promise of a past that can't be reclaimed. For how much I had convinced myself that I hated this man, hearing him say that he used to love me made me crack a bit.

"Marcus, I—" My voice falters, a tremor of uncertainty betraying the resolve I had mustered.

He steps closer, his presence overwhelming the small space between us. It's as if he sees the crumbling edges of my defenses—like a predator sensing the vulnerability of its prey. "Aurora," he whispers, and the sound of my name on his lips is familiar and jarring.

His hand grazes my cheek, a touch feather-light yet laden with intent. He leans in, and his lips meet mine in an apology, a plea, a tether to our entwined past. "I'm sorry," he breathes against my skin. "I need you. We were magic together. Without you, the music... it's just not the same."

The kiss is a question, an offering laced with the honeyed poison of nostalgia. His words are a melody that once pulsed through my veins, but now, they echo hollowly in the chambers of my heart.

"Come back to me," he urges. "Let's create again. Together."

My mind whirls, caught in a tempest of what was and what could be. Langston's face flashes before me—a beacon of warmth and sincerity, contrasting the fraught tension that Marcus weaves. Langston offered me solace, a chance to find myself beyond the shadows of another person's limelight.

But Marcus was offering me a highway to my dream.

"Marcus, I can't just—" I start, the conflict within me spilling into my voice.

"Can't or won't?" he challenges, his fingers trailing down my arm, igniting conflicted emotions.

Images flicker in rapid succession: moments with Langston filled with laughter and quiet understanding, solitary hours spent crafting melodies that were wholly mine, the sharp sting of betrayal each time Marcus overshadowed my voice. The choice before me wasn't as clear as love or career. At one point I did love Marcus. *Could I want to again?*

"Langston... he believes in me," I whisper, though the words feel like a betrayal even as they pass my lips.

"Does he believe in your music? Or does he just believe in the idea of you? How can he understand you like I do?" Marcus's voice is smooth, bent to sound like doubt's cure. His lips graze across my neck, and a hum vibrated my throat before I could cage it.

Marcus' touch was familiar.

An argument outside shatters the fragile stillness of the room. Langston's voice, unmistakable in its controlled urgency, cuts through the air like a blade. My breath catches, the daze Marcus has spun around me dissipating as if it were never there. The touch on my neck now feels invasive, and I instinctively step away, moving toward the commotion.

"Langston?" I call out as I yank open the door.

The scene before me is frozen with tension. Langston stands inches from the towering frame of Marcus's bodyguard, their chests puffed in silent challenge. My name leaves his lips in a half-whisper, half-warning as our eyes lock. In that split second, a myriad of emotions pass between us—fear, concern, agitation.

I see the moment when Langston registered Marcus standing behind me. The look on his face shifts from agitation to anger.

"What's up, professor? Ah, if it isn't the Celestial Sexy Scientist," Marcus sneers with a laugh that carries no humor, only scorn. "Come to rescue your damsel from the big, bad wolf?"

I can sense the tension radiating from Langston. He steps forward, his eyes never leaving Marcus. There's an unspoken battle in their gazes.

"Marcus, stop it," I snap. But it's lost in the standoff before me.

"Look at him," Marcus continues, his tone dripping with condescension. He walks up behind me and holds the door open wider as he looked Langston up and down. "How you think this pencil-pusher gets someone like us? You belong on stage, Aurora. With me."

Before I can interject, before I can explain or defend, Langston's expression shifts from anger to something far more pained. He turns away without a word, his shoulders taut with a mix of defeat and resolve.

"Langston, wait!" I call after him, but he doesn't stop or look back.

"See?" Marcus says behind me, his voice now gentle, coaxing. "You don't need him. We can be great again, you and I."

But his words fall flat, the manipulation now transparent and ugly. My mind races with thoughts of Langston—how he cares, his genuine belief in me.

"Give me some space, Marcus," I manage to say, my voice shaking. "Please, just go."

He hesitates, his eyes searching mine for something—forgiveness, acquiescence, love. But there is none to be found. Eventually, he nods slowly.

"A'ight," he says. There is a subtle shift in his energy. His voice was a bit colder. His mask of fake emotions slipping. "But, Aurora, you need me. That little video you made will be forgotten next week. I'll still be here. And you can be with me where you belong. We got a new album to put together."

He steps into my personal space. "You can pretend you wanna write these songs about this corny dude. But your songs are *our* music. *Ours.* And if you want anyone to hear your songs again, you best remember who wrote your chorus."

He turns and walks away, followed by his hulking guard. The wind whips, and suddenly, I feel a cold right to my bones.

Chapter 9

Langston

Aurora's presence filled the room, her soft breathing starkly contrasting with the tense atmosphere between us.

She'd come to talk to me about a proposal to work together that Marcus had texted her after he left her place.

"Langston," she whispered, "I know you don't want me to work with Marcus again, but I can't just walk away from all I've worked for."

I clenched my fists, anger and fear bubbling inside me. I was mad at her. And I was mad at myself for being mad at her.

At no time had she made a promise to me. And she'd work for years on her dream. We had known each other what, a few weeks? I felt selfish for being mad at her for grabbing an opportunity to fulfill her dream. When I had a chance to follow mine, no one could stop me.

But the thought of her going back to that manipulative man tightened my chest, making it difficult to breathe. "You know what he's capable of, Aurora. You saw firsthand how he tried to control you and take credit for your talent. And he's an asshole."

Tears pooled but didn't fall—the same stubborn defiance that first drew me to her. "Believe me, I know. But if there's even a chance that I can regain my career and prove to the world that it was me behind those songs –" She hesitated, bit her lip, then continued. "I have to take that risk."

"Even if it means letting him back into your life?" I asked, trying to keep my voice steady and devoid of the pain tearing at my heart.

"Only professionally," she insisted, her eyes meeting mine. "Nothing more."

But how could I be sure? From the stories she'd told me, it was clear that Marcus had a way of worming his way into people's lives. And I knew he wouldn't stop until he had her under his thumb again- no matter what her plan was. It wasn't just about her career – it was about control, and I couldn't bear the thought of losing her to someone like him.

"Promise me," I said, strained, "promise me that you'll be careful, that you won't let him manipulate you again."

Aurora stepped forward, closing the distance between us, and touched my chest. "I promise, Langston. I won't let him hurt me again."

I felt the walls around my heart crumbling as I looked into her eyes, searching for any hint of doubt or uncertainty. All I saw was determination and a fierce love that matched my own.

"Alright," I breathed out, pulling her closer. "I trust you." But deep down, I couldn't help but wonder if I was making a grave mistake – risking her career and our future together. I could trust her, but I certainly didn't trust him.

"Thank you, Langston," Aurora whispered, her eyes full of gratitude. "I know it's not easy for you to accept this, but I need to do this for myself, my career, and us."

"Us?" I asked, clinging to the hope that she still saw a future with me despite the storm brewing on the horizon.

"Of course," she replied, her gaze never wavering from mine. "I care about you, and nothing Marcus does or says will change that. Please believe me. But if I don't do everything in my power to be who I know I can because I'm afraid I'll lose whatever this is between us... it might..."

I nodded, swallowing the lump in my throat. "Make you hate me. I get it. And I believe you, Aurora. Just... please be careful. I can't bear the thought of losing you because of him."

Aurora leaned in, pressing her lips against mine in a tender kiss. As much as I wanted to protect her, I knew she had to face this challenge on her terms. She needed to prove strong enough to stand up to Marcus and reclaim her rightful place in the music industry.

"I'll be careful," she murmured against my lips, her breath warm and sweet. "I promise."

It only took one more brush of her lips against mine before I dragged her toward the bed.

My heart pounded against my chest as I removed her top, taking in the sight of her full breasts with awe. Her skin carried salt and vanilla from her lotion, and I couldn't resist tracing my tongue along her collarbone, eliciting a soft moan from her. She shivered, it just made me want to keep going.

She let my hands roam her body, rediscovering her curves and tracing the dips between her shoulder blades and soft hips. She felt like she was piece of a puzzle that clicked right into place with me.

I needed her to know she was safe with me and how much I wanted her. My gentle grazes on her skin got firmer as she pressed her body flush into mine. I kissed down her neck, her giggle dissolved into a gasp when my stubble grazed her throat—a sound that coiled heat low in my gut. I pulled her closer so she could see that her melodious sound made me rock hard.

"It tickles," she chided breathlessly.

"It'll tickle more when I rub it down there," I said quietly as I buried my face into her curls.

Her hands moved my head, pulling me closer as she arched in. And when my lips found hers, she opened to accept my tongue like it was the best thing she ever tasted.

As we fell onto the bed, I pulled off my shirt and pushed her down flat. I was for damn sure gonna make sure her mind was on me the next time she saw that punk, Marcus.

I looked into her eyes, and I squeezed her breasts together. Her buds stood straight up, waiting for my mouth. I took one deep chocolate nipple into my mouth, sucking tenderly while I let my hand squeeze the other one firmly. A soft cry escaped her lips as she arched off the bed. It just made me want to please her more.

She'd been stressed and hadn't shaved in a few days. I kinda liked it. I let my fingers trail along the hairs on her inner thigh. She trembled, her hips bucking up to let me part her folds. I grazed her sensitive area, letting her feel my soft hair on the side of pussy walls before I darted out my tongue to dance over her clit, making her whimper in delight. Her moans were music, and I was gonna make her dance to that tone.

So I grabbed that ass that drove me crazy and buried my head in between her thighs. I licked, sucked, slurped until she was crying for me to show mercy. Her body shuttered with an orgasm, and a beautiful liquid released. And I licked it up while she moaned and bucked.

I left just enough juice to make it nice for her when I slid two fingers inside her tightness.

"Shit, Langston!" Her body pulsed around my fingers. I held her hips hard, never breaking eye contact, moving my fingers to her beautiful sounds until she shuddered another climax.

"What's my fucking name?" I asked her as she cried. She didn't answer, but moved my hands and laid a demand.

"Fuck me, hard."

I didn't need more invitation. I reached for the rubber on the dresser, but she pulled me back. We'd done the test thing. I still just assumed I still wrapped, but apparently I was wrong.

"Raw," she said.

Shit less needed to be said, as I moved over her, between her legs. And in one push, I sank into her warmth inch by gritted inch.. I heard her curse and was about to pull away when she started to mutter.

"Fuck yes. Your name is Langston. My Langston. Fucking star... my fucking star, with that fucking shit I need."

Her words caught me off guard. She didn't usually talk that way. But that shit was sexy. And if it was possible at all, my dick got harder. I pumped that cock full hilt into her over and over, looking at her beautiful face etched in a combination of pain and ecstasy. Her titties bounced in rhythm to my strokes. Her hands scratched my back.

It was too much, and I couldn't hold it any more. I released a full load right on her spot, and she joined me again as we rolled to a climax. I crumbled onto her, and she wrapped me in her arms.

All I could think was that I wasn't ever letting this woman go.

Aurora

As I lay there, curled up in Langston's arms, my heart swelled with love for him. But amidst the warmth and safety of his embrace, a nagging thought kept creeping into my mind – Marcus.

The connection between Langston and me was undeniable; our passion had just been a testament to that. Yet, the fear of losing my career and dreams if I didn't return to work with Marcus gnawed at me. It seemed like an impossible choice.

I sighed. "I care about you, Langston, more than I ever thought possible. But my music... it's a part of me too. And I'm scared that I might lose everything I've fought for if I don't take this opportunity."

Langston held me tighter as if sensing my internal struggle. "Aurora, I feel the same. And I want what's best for you. If working with Marcus will help you achieve your dreams, I'll support you. But promise me one thing: don't let him control you or hurt you again."

I nodded, filled with gratitude for Langston's understanding. "I promise. I won't let Marcus come between us, and I'll make sure our relationship remains purely professional."

My heart felt split between Langston's tenderness and my lifelong ambitions. As I lay in Langston's arms, I knew that no matter what happened, I'd fight to protect our love and my dreams – even if it meant facing Marcus again.

The next morning, I awoke to a text message from Marcus. He asked if I had thought about his offer and wanted to see if I would talk before he flew back to LA. He also invited me to an award ceremony he was nominated for. The gall.

I didn't want to, but it was a conversation that I had to have. Between Langston's support and all the love Aunt Cecily had poured into me, I was stronger than ever, ready to reclaim my career without sacrificing anything of myself.

I left Langston's apartment and went to Marcus' hotel room. My heart raced as I knocked on the door, steeling myself for the conversation ahead. When he opened the door, his eyes glinted with devious charm.

"Ah, Aurora, come in," Marcus said smoothly, gesturing for me to enter. I bristled as I walked past him into the room. Just being near him made my skin crawl.

He gestured for me to take a seat, but I remained standing, arms folded across my chest.

"Marcus, let's get straight to the point," I began, my voice steady despite the emotions swirling within me. "I will *consider* working with you again, but under certain conditions. First, you must publicly acknowledge my contributions to your career and retract all the crap you insinuated about me on social media. Second, our relationship will be strictly professional – nothing more."

He raised an eyebrow, clearly surprised by my assertiveness. His handsome face cracked into a friendly smile. "You drive a hard bargain, Aurora. But if that's what it takes to get you back on my team, I'll agree to your terms."

"Good," I replied, feeling a small victory in standing up for myself. "I want everything in writing before we proceed, and I expect you to honor your word."

"Of course, Aurora," Marcus assured me, though I could see the wheels turning in his mind, calculating his next move. But I refused to be intimidated.

"Additionally," I continued, my resolve growing stronger, "I want it understood that the lawsuit will be dropped *if* you follow through on your promises. No more games, Marcus."

"Fine, fine," he conceded, his smile faltering. "You have my word, Aurora."

"Remember, all of this needs to be in writing," I reminded him. "And one more thing – if you ever try anything inappropriate or unprofessional with me again, I won't hesitate to walk away for good."

"Alright, I understand," Marcus replied, clearly taken aback by my firmness. He raised his hands in mock surrender. "Everything will be as you've requested. I know I've made mistakes in the past, but I want us to move forward and succeed together."

"Thank you," I said tersely. His eyes tracked me as I moved deeper into the room, but still arms crossed.

"Lastly," I added, wrapping up the conversation, "I wanted to address the award ceremony you mentioned. While I appreciate the invitation, I want it to be clear that we are attending as professional colleagues and nothing more. It's the perfect opportunity for you to let the world know all my contributions."

"Of course, Aurora," Marcus responded, his overly nice demeanor still present. "I understand the boundaries you're setting, and I respect them. We'll go as professionals, and I'll make sure our collaboration is publicized so people know we've resolved our differences."

"Alright," I said as I took in his smile stretched too wide – focusing on those same teeth that'd sunk into my career. I knew Marcus well enough to recognize when he was trying too hard to appease me.

"Is there anything else you need from me?" Marcus asked, feigning innocence.

"No," I replied, "That's all for now."

"Great," Marcus said with a smile that didn't quite reach his eyes.

My mind wandered to Tony, who had betrayed me alongside Marcus. I knew I couldn't work with him again, and I needed to make that clear. "Is Tony still your manager?" I asked, trying to keep my voice steady.

"Ah, yes. Tony's still on board," Marcus replied nonchalantly, clearly not expecting the question.

Anger surged inside me, but I did my best to suppress it. My hands clenched into fists as I struggled to hold back my frustration.

Marcus picked up on my reaction and misinterpreted it. A sly smile formed on his lips, and he leaned in closer. "You're jealous, aren't you? You want to get back together, admit it," he taunted, his words dripping with arrogance. "Langston can't give you what I can. He's not cut out for this world. Does he even know how to handle you?"

The mention of Langston snapped me back to reality. A flash of Langston's hurt face from the night before, the words of comfort, the promises, the way he made me feel. It all came back. "No, Marcus, you're wrong. I love Langston." The words hung between us like shattered glass.

Marcus straightened the large watch on his wrist as he attempted to mask his disappointment. "If you write the title song for me, I'll provide the contract. Then we'll see about your little solo thing."

"Good," I retorted rudely. "You are an unlikeable ass, and I want nothing to do with you, privately or personally. We can be seen publicly together, and I'll attend the ceremony, but that's where it ends."

"Alright," Marcus relented, his pride wounded. "I understand. Tony's secretary will contact you with the details, but you won't have to deal with Tony directly."

"Perfect," I said. As I turned to leave, my resolve strengthened; I was ready to navigate the challenges that awaited me, even if I had to dance through firestorms for my music.

Chapter 10

Aurora

The flash of cameras blinded me as we stepped out of the sleek black limousine. My heart pounded in my chest like a trapped bird. The crowd's clamor and reporters' shouted questions churned dizziness in my stomach. This was nothing like the small performance venues I was accustomed to. I had avoided all the stuff like this because I hated it.

The red carpet stretched like a crimson sea, and I was utterly lost in its vastness.

"Smile." Marcus' breath scalded my earlobe. I forced a smile onto my lips, though it was unnatural and uncomfortable. We made our way down the carpet, posing for photos and answering endless questions about our relationship. My voice tremored with each response, betraying my anxiety.

"Tell us, Aurora, how long have you known Marcus?" one reporter asked, her microphone thrust into my face.

"Um, we've known each other since college," I stammered, trying to maintain my composure.

"Are you two officially together? We heard rumors," another reporter chimed in, eager to get the scoop on our personal lives.

I glanced at Marcus, who offered only a coy grin in response. "We're just here to support each other's careers," I managed to say, hoping that would satisfy their curiosity. But I knew it wouldn't be. They wanted more; they wanted a story, a tale of love and passion that would captivate their readers. And I couldn't give them what they wanted.

As we continued along the red carpet, I couldn't help but feel like a fraud. Here I was, dressed in a stunning gown that hugged my curves, standing beside a man whose charm and good looks seemed to captivate everyone around him, and yet I felt like an imposter in my own life. A sequined glove touched my arm – an actress I loved – her Botox mask unable to mirror my trapped scream. She gave me a hug as if were old friends, and the cameras flashed around us. Did I belong in this world of glitz and glamour, or was I just playing a part in someone else's story?

"Come on, Aurora," Marcus urged, tight grip on my waist as if to anchor me to him. "We're almost there."

I nodded, swallowing hard to keep my emotions at bay. Even when we were together, I rarely attended industry parties or ceremonies. That is probably part of why it was so easy for Marcus to be a dirty dog. But I had agreed to this... public appearance. *Ugh.*

We made our way further along the carpet, stopping for more photos and interviews, each one leaving me feeling more exposed and vulnerable than the last.

"Smile, Aurora," Marcus whispered as we navigated through the crowd of eager reporters and fans. "You're going to be fine."

I forced a smile. The sexy, revealing dress I wore only added to my discomfort. That blasted wardrobe stylist Marcus worked with had chosen it for me – showing too much cleavage and constricting around my hips. It was nothing like my usual style, and I felt exposed.

Yet, when I'd shown Langston the outfit during our video call earlier, he seemed to love it. He showered me with compliments, telling me how beautiful and confident I looked.

But as I stood beside Marcus now, Langston's warm words crumbled to ash in this media inferno. The frenzy intensified, their eyes on me, judging me, scrutinizing my every move.

"Are you two officially a couple? Come on now. There was talk when you were in his band," one reporter asked us boldly, thrusting a microphone in our faces.

His band? The phrase detonated in my brain.

"Absolutely," Marcus replied, his grin broadening. "We're very happy together."

"Actually," I interjected, my voice shaking slightly. "We're just here as friends tonight. We're supporting each other professionally."

A hush fell over the small group of reporters that had gathered around us. Marcus's face tightened, and though he didn't say anything, I could sense the anger simmering beneath his calm facade.

"Let's go inside," Marcus said tersely, guiding me away from the reporters and towards the venue entrance. His strong hand was just a bit too tight around my waist. As we walked, I couldn't shake that I'd made a grave error by agreeing to accompany him to this event.

Was I sacrificing the man who understood me for one who saw me as little more than a prop in his own story?

We found our assigned seats inside the venue among other industry professionals and celebrities. The air buzzed with anticipation, excitement, and whispers of gossip as we exchanged tense glances, keenly aware of the scrutiny we were under.

To people who knew Marcus, I probably looked vaguely familiar. That and all the news about a lawsuit and allegations meant everyone wanted to know exactly who I was.

As the award ceremony began, my anxiety grew, and I struggled to focus on the event. I stole glances at Marcus. He looked entirely at home. His slick black tuxedo was accented with a huge diamond earring and black and silver aviator glasses that looked good, but really were ridiculous on anyone not cosplaying 2003 Usher. But to say he wasn't one of the most attractive things in the room would be a lie. He smelled like masculine sex, and I shifted onto my other hip to give myself as much space as possible.

The room was filled with glamorous people – rappers dripping in diamonds, singers draped in luxurious fabrics, models with impossibly long legs, and actors wearing perfectly tailored suits. The dazzling display of wealth and success was both exhilarating and intimidating.

My internal dialogue raced as I took in the spectacle around me. On one hand, I was excited to be in attendance, surrounded by many talented individuals I admired. But on the other hand, I couldn't shake the thought that I didn't belong here, that I was an outsider in this world of glitz and glamour.

"Are you okay?" Marcus asked, his voice low and tinged with irritation.

"Fine." My smile felt stapled on. "I'm just a little overwhelmed."

"Try to enjoy yourself," he said. His gaze crawled over glittering attendees. "You deserve to be here, Aurora. And smile, damn it, you're on camera."

"Thanks." I replied, the lies he told curdled my stomach.

As the ceremony continued, I found myself lost in thought, questioning my choices and wondering what the future held for me.

Throughout the ceremony, Marcus and I were subjected to whispers and speculative glances from those around us. I couldn't enjoy any performances as I sensed the judgmental eyes on me. The scrutiny made me question whether my budding relationship with Langston could withstand this pressure.

I stole a glance at Marcus, who seemed unfazed by the attention. He exuded confidence and control while I struggled to maintain my composure. I was uncomfortable. He knew I would be. It's probably why he wanted me here--to see me squirm.

During a break in the ceremony, I excused myself to get a drink. I needed a moment away from the prying eyes and whispered judgments. As I approached the bar area, my heart skipped a beat when I found myself face-to-face with Tony, Marcus' manager.

"Nice to see you again, Aurora," he said, his voice dripping with sarcasm. His gaze was cold, and his lips curled into a subtle smirk. My skin crawled under his predatory stare.

"Tony," I replied, trying to keep my tone even, as if his presence didn't bother me.

"Enjoying the show?" he asked, his eyes never leaving mine.

"Of course," I responded, struggling to keep my voice steady. "It's quite the event."

"Indeed," he agreed, taking a sip of his drink. "And quite the spectacle you and Marcus are making. Stirring up quite a bit of talk, aren't you?"

"Is there something you want, Tony?" I asked, growing increasingly agitated by his insinuations.

"Only to wish you luck, Aurora," he replied, his smile widening into a sinister grin. "You're going to need it."

With that, he sauntered away, leaving me feeling shaken and rattled. My heart pounded in my chest as I gripped the edge of the bar counter, trying to regain my composure. What did Tony mean? Was he trying to undermine my confidence or hinting at something more sinister in store for me?

As I settled back into my seat, Marcus immediately made small gestures of physical affection, like placing his hand on mine and putting his arm around me. I felt a surge of annoyance at his actions. If we were in private, I'd kick him in the nuts— but Marcus was taking advantage of our public appearance to break our agreement. I wished he would just respect my boundaries, but it seemed like an impossible ask. So, lost in my thoughts, I hardly registered the moment when Marcus' name was announced from the stage. He stood and pulled me in for a passionate, forceful kiss. He slid two arms around me and plunged his tongue deep without permission - a wet invasion broadcast live.

I broke away from him, my eyes wide with shock. Looking around, I realized that a TV camera was right in our faces. Marcus had won the award, and the whole thing was televised. My cheeks burned with embarrassment and anger as whispers and murmurs rippled through the crowd.

Marcus lowered his glasses enough to give me a wink, then sauntered to the stage, the TV camera trailing behind him. I struggled to keep my composure after the forced public display of affection Marcus had subjected me to.

As Marcus took the stage, his smile gleaming under the spotlights, he launched into his acceptance speech. He thanked a host of people for helping him with his last album, each name punctuating my growing frustration and disbelief. When he mentioned Tony, a wave of disgust washed over me. But what hurt the most was that Marcus didn't mention me at all. I had poured my soul into our collaboration, yet he completely disregarded my contributions.

Overwhelmed by the eyes on me, the murmurs, and the embarrassment, I rushed to take a moment to myself in the restroom. The cool, dim space offered a brief reprieve from the event's intensity. As I looked at myself in the mirror, my reflection stared back, tears welling in my eyes. I had let Marcus back into my life, and he'd screwed me again. I knew it was going to happen. And I let it. So, was it really all his fault?

Langston

I watched the award ceremony unfold on the screen before me, my eyes narrowing as I saw Aurora's discomfort with Marcus' public displays of affection. Hands around her waist, lips whispering in her ear. It was making me sick.

"Damn it," I muttered under my breath, clenching my fist. The channel I was watching showed the red carpet moments. There was a sea of bodies, but all I could pay attention to was Aurora's forced smile as she posed for the cameras and her jaw tight as Marcus grabbed every interviewer's mic that tried reaching her lips.. Clearly, she was unhappy, but she kept up appearances for the event's sake.

Why did she agree to go with him in the first place? I couldn't help but feel a pang of fear that the glamour and fame of this lifestyle might lure her away from me. That she would choose Marcus and his world over our love. I shook my head, trying to dispel those thoughts. We had built something genuine and beautiful together, hadn't we?

"Get a grip, Langston," I whispered, taking a deep breath.

I thought back to our video call earlier that night. Aurora had shown me the sexy, dress she wore for the event. The crimson dress hugged her curves perfectly - plunging neckline meeting thigh-high slit in one dangerous line. She looked stunning, but I could see the uncertainty in her eyes.

"Langston, I don't know... I'm scared I don't look good in this dress," she confessed, biting her lip nervously. "I'll just look and sound stupid on the red carpet. I mean, there will be models on there. What do I look like wearing this next to them?"

"Are you kidding?" I replied, trying to reassure her. "You look gorgeous, Aurora. Breathtaking. Trust me, no one will be able to take their eyes off of you." Our conversation soon turned playful as we flirted despite the distance between us. She'd only left two days ago, and I'd spoken to her several times a day, but I still missed her.

My thoughts returned to the present, watching the award ceremony on TV. I realized how little I knew about the world Aurora came from. Many of the people there were strangers to me, though they seemed to be well-known celebrities. I wondered if I would feel out of place if I attended an event like this with her in the future. My academic events paled compared to the glitz and glamour of these red-carpet affairs. Still, most high-level academics brought certain *kind* of people as their dates to our events--namely, other "egg heads," as Malcolm called them. One time, since I didn't want to take a date to a ceremony I was getting an award at, I had brought Malcolm. Three times I caught him pretending to fall asleep while standing up next to me as I chatted with colleagues. He said he'd never go to another one. Would she fit in at those? Or would it drive a wedge between us?

As my worries swirled, I tried to focus on the love we shared and the connection that brought us together. We might come from different worlds, but we found solace in each other's arms.

As I watched the show, I noticed each time the camera panned to show Marcus and Aurora, he was getting closer and closer, initiating small public displays of affection. I felt a physical ache as I saw her discomfort, and anger began to bubble up inside me. His hand on hers. His arm around her chair. I know he'd agreed they weren't together, but he was trying shit cause they were in public.

"Damn him," I muttered under my breath.

Soon enough, Marcus was announced as the winner of an Up And Coming Artist Award. It was at that moment when things took a turn for the worse. Marcus yanked Aurora into frame - one hand sliding from hipbone to chest claim-stake as his mouth crashed down. The audacity of his actions made my red haze descend, and I couldn't help but yell and curse in my living room.

"Son of a bitch!" I screamed at the television, my voice hoarse with rage.

Aurora immediately pushed Marcus away, a furious expression on her face. It was clear she hadn't expected it either, but the damage was done. I continued to fume as I listened to Marcus' speech, my anger only growing when he failed to mention Aurora.

Of course, I thought. *She's just another accessory to him.*

As the award ceremony continued, I paced restlessly in my living room. I needed to talk to Aurora—to reassure her that we could get through this together.

But first, I had to calm down and collect my thoughts.

As I tried to regain my composure, my phone rang, jolting me out of my thoughts. The caller ID showed Malcolm's name, and I quickly answered the call.

"Man, have you been watching this?" Malcolm barked. No hello, just straight to anger.

"Unfortunately," I replied bitterly. "I can't believe what Marcus just did, shit."

"Tell me about it," Malcolm agreed, equally upset. "It's clear he's only trying to embarrass Aurora and force her back into working with him. And by laying claim to her on national TV like that, he's making it seem like she has no other choice. I promise if I ever see that dude-"

I realized Malcolm was right. Marcus had concocted this entire spectacle to trap Aurora, undermining any legitimacy to her claims that she was gathering and any progress we'd made in our relationship. My anger grew even more intense.

"Damn him! He's not going to get away with this. I won't let him manipulate Aurora and ruin her life again," I declared, my voice shaking with determination.

"Listen, Langston, you need to talk to Aurora. She needs your support now more than ever. Don't let Marcus win," Malcolm advised, his tone serious.

"You're right," I agreed, taking a deep breath to calm myself. "I'm going to call her now and make sure she knows I'm here for her, no matter what."

"Good," Malcolm said. "And remember, you two are stronger together than apart. Plus you got 'ol boy. I'll help you whenever, however. You know that, man."

"Thanks, man. I needed to hear that," I replied gratefully before hanging up.

As soon as I disconnected the call, I took a moment to let Malcolm's words sink in. He was right - we couldn't let Marcus win. Aurora and I had something special, something real, and I wasn't about to let him destroy it.

But Malcolm's warning about the backlash weighed heavily on my mind. The thought of being thrust into the public eye, with everyone scrutinizing our relationship and questioning my reaction to the kiss, made me uneasy. My privacy was important to me, and I couldn't help but worry that this newfound attention would overshadow my academic career. I wanted to be known as Professor Wilkerson, the guy who unlocked a mystery of the universe. One day as a Nobel Laureate. Not this.

I glanced at my phone, knowing I needed to talk to Aurora. But I hesitated, my fingers hovering over her contact. What could I even say to her? How could I reassure her when I was unsure how to navigate the mess that Marcus had created?

As I was lost in thought, my phone rang again, the screen displaying an unknown number. Reluctantly, I answered it, steeling myself for whatever conversation might come.

"Hello, is this Langston Wilkerson? This is Tina from Gossip Central. We'd like your reaction to the kiss between Aurora and Marcus tonight at the award ceremony. How do you feel about what happened?"

My jaw clenched, and anger bubbled up inside me. I couldn't believe that a gossip journalist had already tracked me down, eager to dig into my personal life. "I have nothing to say to you," I growled before abruptly hanging up the phone.

Frustration surged through me as I realized Malcolm had been right – the media wouldn't waste time sinking their teeth into this story. And if they had found me, there was no doubt they would be hounding Aurora, too. The thought of her enduring even more unwanted attention fueled my determination to contact her.

"Dammit," I muttered under my breath as I pulled up her contact and hit 'call.' The phone rang several times, each tone increasing my anxiety, but there was no answer. I tried again, hoping she would pick up, but still no response.

With every unanswered call, my concern grew. I could only imagine how overwhelmed she must be– the media frenzy, Marcus's betrayal, and now likely being bombarded by reporters. My heart ached for her, and I desperately wished I was by her side to support her through this ordeal.

"Please, Aurora," I whispered into the empty air, willing her to pick up the phone. "Just let me know you're okay."

As I tried reaching her, I couldn't help but think about the uncertainty ahead for both of us. But one thing was clear – I wouldn't let Marcus's manipulations tear us apart. No matter our challenges, I was determined to fight for Aurora and our love.

Chapter 11

Aurora

The antiseptic airport chill seeped into my pores, but I could still feel the heat of the humiliation from the night before. I sat in an inconspicuous corner of the crowded terminal, shrouded in the anonymity of oversized sweatpants and a hoodie. The dark glasses perched on my nose were both a shield and a cage—protecting me from prying eyes while confining me with recursive anxieties.

Memories of the award ceremony flickered like a faulty projector in my mind. Marcus's grip on my hand had seemed so reassuring, his smile so convincing. I had allowed myself to believe, for one treacherous moment, that he might actually acknowledge me—the music we'd birthed together and the soul I'd poured into it. Yet, as he accepted the accolade, his words danced around everyone but me. I was a ghost, present but unseen.

And that kiss. That damn kiss, on national television.

I should have known better than to trust Marcus. The vultures were waiting with their cameras and questions as soon as we left. They followed me back to where I was staying, some even arriving before I got there. I had to sneak out to get away from them when I arranged to catch an earlier flight.

It was more than just my pride that had been injured; it was my claim, my right to the artistry that had flowed from my veins into our music. With every breathless second that he held me close on what looked like a date, my contributions slipped further away, unclaimed and unrecognized.

A knot tightened in my stomach as I considered social media's cruel court of public opinion. I could almost hear the whispers and jeers behind the glowing screens, casting judgment without care or context. I imagined my name, once again, being dragged through the virtual mud, my story twisted by those who knew nothing of its truth.

The reality was clear: I had taken a blow in this fight. But beneath the layers of doubt and sorrow, a faint spark of defiance still flickered. It was the part of me that refused to be silenced and diminished—the same ember that ignited my music with passion and pain.

As the hum of conversation and announcements swirled around me, I closed my eyes and leaned back against the stiff airport seat. Inside, the storm of emotions raged on, a tempest seeking escape through the melodies thrumming beneath fractured nerves, begging to be set free. In this moment of stillness, Langston's star charts mapped across my eyelids. So vast, so beautiful. And my problems shrunk, if just for but a moment.

"Flight 247 to Chicago, boarding at gate B12, has been delayed," the intercom's static-laced voice interrupted the storm of my thoughts. I huffed a deep breath. All I wanted was to get out of here.

My phone vibrated insistently again, and this time, it was Aunt Cecily's number that lit up the screen. She, Langston, and a few others who cared had been trying to reach me since last night, but their concern was a weight I wasn't ready to carry—not until I could make sense of the mess in my own head.

With hesitant fingers, I swiped to decline, then crafted a message to Aunt Cecily, letting her know I was on my way back, "Leaving soon. Coming back to Chicago. Will explain everything over tea then." I sent the text with a promise of a conversation I dreaded yet desperately needed. Aunt Cecily, with her eccentric wisdom, would have words that could guide me, even if they couldn't immediately heal the open wounds.

My phone rang just as I slipped it back into the pocket of my hoodie. The number was unfamiliar, a string of digits without a name to anchor them. Curiosity wrestled with caution, but the former won out as it often did. I wiped my palms on my sweatpants and answered, "Hello?"

"Is this Aurora?" The voice on the other end was careful and measured—familiar yet difficult to place.

"Speaking. Who is this?"

There was a pause, a breath taken on the other side of the line as if gathering strength. "It's Maria. Tony's wife."

Maria. Her image came to mind unbidden: quiet, composed, the solid foundation upon which the talent management firm operated while Tony played the charismatic front man. Our interactions had always been cordial, straightforward—decent.

"Maria," I said, my voice steadying out of respect for her. "How can I help you?"

"Help me?" A soft, bitter chuckle fluttered through the connection. "It seems we might be in a position to help each other."

I shifted uncomfortably, pressing the phone closer to my ear as travelers swarmed around me, oblivious to the conversation. "What do you mean?"

"Let's just say I've had enough," she replied, her tone hushed but laced with an intensity that demanded attention. "Enough of the lies, the manipulation... of being overshadowed by those who think they're smarter than us."

I swallowed, the airport's noise fading into the background as her words resonated within me. It was a shared sentiment, a common ground forged in the fires of betrayal.

"Maria, what are you talking about? What happened?"

"Last night," she began, and the gravity in her voice anchored me to the spot, "was the final straw."

"I was there last night when Marcus kissed you. Live on television."

I remembered the sting of humiliation afresh, a public spectacle I had no part in orchestrating. I remained silent, and she took this as a sign to continue.

"Yesterday I overheard Tony and Marcus talking," Maria confided, her voice dropping to a conspiratorial murmur. "Scheming about something big, something that would grab everyone's attention. But I didn't know..." She trailed off, the silence heavy between us.

"Didn't know what they planned for the whole world to see," I finished for her.

"Exactly. And I want you to know, Aurora," Maria's voice grew firmer, "how repulsed I am by their actions. By this... circus they've created. I didn't get into this business for this shit show."

It was hard to digest, coming from someone so integral to the very firm that had become part of the source of my anguish. "Maria, when I came to you last year, when I told you about Tony and Marcus--"

The words caught in my throat, a lump forming as I remembered the betrayal.

"About them sleeping together?" Maria cut in, her tone matter-of-fact. "Yes, I remember. You must understand, my marriage with Tony... we have an understanding. An open relationship. So technically, my husband wasn't cheating."

"Technically," I echoed, the word tasting sour on my tongue.

"Be a big girl, Aurora" she said softly. "I had the relationship with my husband that I wanted. I knew about Tony's, er, wide tastes. I understand you and Marcus didn't have an understanding, so they did you dirty. I may not have been cheated on in the traditional sense, but believe me that I've been betrayed in every other way imaginable. By both of them."

Her confession hung in the air, a shared acknowledgment of wounds inflicted by the same blade. It was a strange comfort, knowing that despite our different circumstances, Maria and I were bound by a common thread of deception.

"Maria," I whispered, my voice barely carrying over the bustling terminal. "What are you planning to do?"

"Tony's dirty methods, his underhanded dealings," she declared, her voice laced with resolute disgust. "--that's not how I envisioned our business." There was a pause, and when she continued, her words were sharp with raw indignation. "And Marcus—ignoring our contributions like we're nothing but footnotes in his success story. Neither of us was mentioned in his acceptance speech, Aurora. He had praise for Tony, his fuck buddy, but not the woman who actually crafted his lucrative deals."

I clenched the phone tighter, feeling the sting of invisibility that crept up every time Marcus smiled for the cameras, basking in unearned adulation. The betrayal seared through me, acidic and relentless.

"Marcus and Tony," Maria continued, her voice dropping to a conspiratorial whisper, "they're still together. And after what I found them doing at my house, which Tony knows is never a location option for escapades, while they were laughing about how they embarrassed you... it's unforgivable."

My heart raced, each beat a hammer against my ribcage. They had been laughing at my expense. The humiliation from last night's charade burned anew, and my breaths came out ragged and sharp.

"Maria, what did you find?" The question slipped out, dread coiling in my stomach.

"Doesn't matter," she replied briskly. "What matters is that I am done. I'm filing for divorce, and I won't be working with Tony any longer. You see, Aurora..." Her tone shifted, and there was a weight to her next words. "I am the controlling interest in the talent management business through a GRAT trust established pre-marriage, not Tony. He's always been the face, but I've been the foundation."

The revelation hit me like a wave, unexpected and overwhelming. I remember going to her office once and seeing all those diplomas and a fancy certificate from passing the Bar. Maria, the quiet force behind the scenes, held the power all along.

"Here's my proposal," Maria said, her voice now imbued with a new determination. "I want to start fresh. And I want you, Aurora, to be the first artist I sign. You have a gift, a real talent that deserves to be shared with the world on your terms."

Her belief in me was a buoy in the stormy sea of my thoughts. Could this be the lifeline I needed? A chance to break free from the tangle of Marcus and everything he represented?

"Maria, I—" My words faltered, a mix of hope and trepidation knotting inside me.

"Think about it," she urged. "But don't take too long. When I file for divorce next week and start separating my business from Tony, it will all go public. I'd like to control the narrative and benefit from exposure boost the media explosion will make by announcing you as an officially signed artist at the same time. And yes, pour some salt into the wound of those two bastards when they realize I'm leaving them high and dry and taking you with me. The two talented women behind them combined and winning without them."

"Okay," I managed, my head spinning with possibilities and fears. "I'll think about it."

"Good," Maria replied, a hint of warmth returning to her voice. "Remember, Aurora, you're stronger than you know."

We ended the call, and I sat there, alone amidst the crowd. Slipping deeper into the anonymity provided by my hoodie and glasses, I let the noise of the bustling terminal wash over me as I retreated into the recesses of my mind. My thoughts drifted back to Marcus, his image conjured up like a specter from a song I wished I could forget.

The emotional abuse I had endured under his guise of 'love' resurfaced—his harsh words, the subtle put-downs that chipped away at my self-esteem, the way he'd dismiss my ideas only to parade them as his own. He'd twisted my passion, my art, into a tool for his ascent, leaving me in the shadows, questioning my worth and doubting my talent.

I remembered the nights I'd spent cradling my guitar, pouring my soul into melodies that he would claim credit for. How could I have been so blind? How did I allow him to convince me that his success was ours when, in reality, it was always about him—and only him?

I couldn't think about Maria's offer clearly. All I knew was that I needed to hear Langston's voice—to seek solace in his unwavering support.

With trembling fingers, I dialed his number.

"Langston, it's me," I said, a soft sigh escaping me at the sound of his name. "I'm at the airport, coming home."

Langston

The phone buzzed like a trapped hornet against my skull, relentless and distracting. I'd been trying to reach Aurora since last night's spectacle at the award ceremony. Each ringtone was a reminder that she hadn't answered, and neither had her aunt Cecily.

"Professor Wilkerson," one of my students called out, snapping me back to the present as I stood in the midst of a lecture hall filled with eager minds. "What do you think about the black hole information paradox? It's weird they borrow our terms to explain stuff like that."

"Ah, yes," I replied, steering my thoughts away from the black hole of personal drama to celestial equations waiting on the board. "It's a bit odd, but it makes sense. Information is not lost; it's simply transformed. Much like our experiences, they shape us, even when they seem to disappear."

But my heart wasn't in it. My research on celestial mechanics felt trivial compared to the chaos around Aurora. After the ceremony, images of her locked in an unexpected embrace with Marcus had flooded every social media feed, igniting a wildfire of speculation.

I could sense my student's eyes on me, questions lurking behind their studious facades. They wanted to know if I was the cuckolded lover, the forgotten man in the drama of the celebrity world. It was unsettling how quickly personal boundaries evaporated under the heat of public scrutiny.

"Professor?" another student prodded, sensing my distraction.

"Apologies," I muttered, shaking off the annoyance. "Let's get back to the event horizon."

As the class ended and the students filed out, I was left with the weight of anticipation. I needed to hear from her. The academic corridors, once a sanctuary of intellectual pursuit, now were oppressive, the whispers of colleagues like gravitational waves distorting my peace.

Even college professors gossiped. I couldn't wait to get back to my office.

The door to my office creaked open, and Jamal stepped in, a bright-eyed contrast to the dull ache of worry that had taken up residence in my chest. He was all youthful enthusiasm and earnestness—a walking embodiment of hope in the midst of my disquiet.

"Professor Wilkerson," he said, his voice genuine, "you hear the nonsense they're spewing? Don't sweat it. Anyone gabbing about you doesn't know the first thing."

I offered him a half-smile, appreciating his loyalty. Jamal wasn't just another student; he was a reminder of where I came from and what I aspired to give back to my community. He flipped his glasses down and took a seat.

"Thanks, Jamal. It means a lot." I leaned back in my chair, embracing the measure of comfort in his solidarity.

His face lit up with an aspirational glow as he continued, "One day, I want to be like you—making big discoveries, respected... and hopefully, with someone like Aurora by my side too. I saw her picture from last night. She fine as shit-" He caught himself mid-word. "Er, sorry. No disrespect, professor."

I couldn't help but chuckle. I mean he wasn't wrong.

"Love makes string theory look linear," I said, a tinge of irony in my tone. "Sometimes, even when you think you've figured out all the variables, it surprises you."

He nodded, understanding more than I expected.

"By the way," Jamal added with a touch of eagerness, "thanks for putting in that referral for the fellowship grant. Just waiting on the news now."

"Of course, Jamal. You deserve every chance at success," I encouraged, proud of his ambition. He was the future, and moments like this reassured me that my work went beyond blackboards and theories.

As our conversation lulled, the sharp trill of my phone cut through the silence of the office. My heart leaped into my throat as I saw Aurora's name flash across the screen. Excitement mingled with concern, fusing into a potent cocktail that made my hands tremble slightly as I reached for the call.

"Hey, I gotta go, Professor," Jamal said, reading the urgency in my movement. "Good luck."

"Thank you, Jamal," I managed before he slipped out, closing the door behind him with a soft click.

Alone now, with the walls seemingly leaning in, I pressed the phone to my ear. "Aurora?"

"Langston..." Her voice dissolved the static in my nerves like antimatter annihilating particles, Just hearing her voice allowed me to breathe easier. "I'm at the airport, coming home."

"Are you okay?" I asked, my tone laced with both excitement and trepidation.

"I'm... I don't even know how to answer that, Langston. I'm sorry for everything," she started, her voice quivering with the weight of unshed tears.

"Stop, Aurora. None of this is your fault," I interrupted. "You've been manipulated and mistreated by people who should've had your back."

She sighed deeply, the sound traveling through the line like a gentle but troubled breeze. "Maria, Tony's wife and partner in the management firm... she called me, Langston. She told me about Tony and Marcus--that it had been planned. And she made me an offer."

"An offer?" I prompted, my curiosity piqued.

"Maria wants to sign me as her first artist. She's leaving Tony, taking control of the management firm," Aurora explained, her words tumbling out as if they were burning her tongue.

"Wow." The news hit me like a meteor strike, sudden and impactful. I took a moment to collect my thoughts, tracing the spines of the books on my shelf with my eyes before speaking again. "Aurora, you know how talented you are. How much your music means—not just to you, but to others."

"Langston, it's scary. I've been under Marcus's shadow for so long, doubting myself..." Her voice trailed off into uncertainty. "I was technically signed with Tony, but I realize that was just a shut-me-up deal."

"Listen to me," I said, my tone soft but insistent. "This could be the break you've been fighting for. A chance to step into the light and show the world the star you are."

"Really? But what if—"

"No 'what ifs'," I cut in. "You've been held down, told you're less than you are. This is your opportunity to rise, Aurora. Maria believes in you, and so do I."

I could almost hear her mind turning over each word, weighing them against the fear that had become her familiar companion.

"Thank you, Langston. That means more than you know." Her breath gusted across three thousand miles of fiber optics.

"Anytime, Aurora. You're not alone in this. Remember that."

"Okay. I'll think about it," she finally said, her voice stronger than it was moments ago.

"Good. Just don't take too long deciding. You deserve happiness and success," I encouraged.

"Thanks, Langston. I needed to hear that," she replied, gratitude warming her tone.

"Actually," she continued, "Do you think I could stay with you for a while? Your place has a door man, and it's not on the first floor where people can look in. Aunt Cecily's walkup might as well have glass walls, and the paparazzi are relentless."

I couldn't suppress the surge of excitement that bubbled up within me. My fingertips found the Newton's cradle on my desk... its silent click-clack keeping time with my pulse. She needed a safe space, and I was it.

"Of course, you can stay with me," I said eagerly, the anticipation clear in my voice. "My doorman don't play, so it's secure. You'll have all the privacy you need."

"Thank you, Langston," she said, relief painting every syllable. "I can't tell you how much it means to have somewhere safe to land."

"Anything for you, Aurora. Just let me know when your flight gets in, and I'll be there." The words tumbled out in a rush, my usual composure slipping in the wave of emotion that her trust invoked.

"I will," she promised. "See you soon."

"Safe travels, Aurora. I'll be waiting," I assured her before we ended the call.

The line went silent, but the echo of her voice lingered, filling the room with the soft melody of our connection. I leaned back in my chair, allowing myself a moment of contemplation. Aurora was coming back—to the city, to her music, and maybe, just maybe, a step closer to me.

Chapter 12

Langston

The soft clacking of the keyboard filled the stillness of the early Sunday morning as I sat hunched over the kitchen counter, my mind threading through the details of Jamal's community outreach project. A few days had slipped by since Aurora's return to Chicago – a city that seemed to breathe easier with her presence. The edges of dawn cast a pale light through the windows, playing across the scattered papers and notes that bore witness to a young man's ambition.

Pride swelled within me, a warm sensation that banished the lingering chill of the apartment. Jamal had done it; he'd secured a fellowship to plan and implement a science outreach program. His proposal sparked the interest of the board that decided which programs the university would get behind. The university had pledged first-year funding, though I suspected alumni donors would ensure continuation beyond that initial commitment. Jamal could stay in school because the grant would pay him to run the program. I was proud. It wasn't just about the money or the recognition. It was about the doors he was opening, not only for himself but for the kids in our old neighborhood who saw their futures in the stars or some other science field, but thought those dreams out of reach.

The idea was brilliant – transforming curiosity into capability, guiding inner-city youth through the labyrinth of hard sciences. His plan deserved more than a cursory glance; it demanded dedication, a nurturing hand to guide it from concept to reality. And I was honored that he wanted me to mentor him as he set it up. I was oddly excited about the opportunity of trying to piece together a roadmap for success, to give these kids a glimpse of what they could achieve.

In moments like this, the gap between my world and theirs seemed bridgeable, the chasm of disconnect that often haunted me less daunting. Maybe this was my way of reconciling the two halves of my existence, of proving that my heart beat in rhythm with the pulse of the streets, even as my head soared among celestial bodies and theories of the universe.

Somewhere across town right now, a kid shooting baskets at the playground was more fascinated with the stars in the sky than the ones on the court. And I wanted them to know that it was completely cool for them to ignite that fire.

As the sun climbed higher, its rays spilling over the countertops, I leaned back in my chair, stretching muscles grown tight with concentration. Morning silence magnified every productive keystroke until Aurora's footsteps disrupted my flow.

I looked up to see her entering the kitchen, her hair a wild halo around her face. She wore an oversized t-shirt that hung off one shoulder, giving her an air of relaxed sensuality that left me breathless. As she smiled at me, a warmth spread through my chest, and I couldn't help but return the smile.

"Morning," she murmured, rubbing her eyes as she padded over to the coffee maker. "What are you working on so early?"

"Hey, beautiful," I replied, allowing my gaze to linger on her for a moment before turning back to my laptop. "I'm helping Jamal. He is launching a community project idea backed by the University. He wants to encourage inner-city kids to explore careers in science."

"Wow." Aurora studied my laptop screen through steam curls rising from her mug. "That's really amazing, Langston. You two are going to make such a difference in their lives."

My cheeks warm at her praise, and I ducked my head slightly, trying to hide the sudden shyness that often seemed to surface with her compliments. I really wasn't used to a woman I was into giving me praise for my work. "I hope so," I admitted, glancing back up at her. "These kids deserve a chance to see that there's more to life than what they've been exposed to."

Her expression softened, and she reached out to place a hand on my forearm, squeezing gently. "This is really good," she said earnestly. "No one even suggested something like this to me when I was in school."

"Thanks," I replied, grateful for her support and encouragement. I mean, I had lived it. A few times I was asked to speak at career days. Each time, when the auditorium or classroom full of kids took in my large muscular frame draped in similar brands to what they'd see basketball stars sporting on the way into a game, though in colors much more toned down, there was an assumption about what I did for a living. When I said I was an astrophysicist, there was usually a look of confusion, then peaked interest. A scientist who looked like them, their brother, father, or guy from the neighborhood.

You a black scientist? A what kind of scientist?

You grew up poor in the hood?

Is that a diamond chain on your necklace?

Is that a gold cap on your tooth? (I only sported it some times a night, but loved wearing it when I went to talk to high school students.)

What kinda scientist listens to rap music?

Bruh said six figures scanning stars? a sophomore had once choked out.

I'd heard it all. Thinking back to a few encounters made me chuckle to myself. By the time I was done with any talk, those kids knew that there was a whole set of opportunities open to them that they might not have considered.

"Langston, I think you'd be an amazing role model for these kids," Aurora said, her eyes filled with sincerity. "You're living proof that they can succeed in the sciences and still stay true to their roots."

I couldn't help but smile at her enthusiasm. "You think so? I've done some speaking engagements at local schools, but maybe I could do more."

"Definitely," she affirmed. "You have a unique perspective and approach that would resonate with them. You'd be able to inspire so many young minds."

"Alright," I nodded. "I'll talk to Jamal about getting more involved. Thanks for your encouragement, Aurora."

"Of course," she smiled warmly. "Now, speaking of encouragement, I've been thinking a lot about Maria's offer to sign me as her client."

"Have you made a decision?" I asked, genuinely curious.

Aurora took a deep breath. "Yes, I've decided to sign with her. She's shown me that a world of opportunity is waiting for me, and I'm ready to embrace it."

"I'm proud of you, Aurora." I meant every word. "It takes courage to step out like this, and I know you'll soar to new heights."

"Thank you," she replied, her eyes sparkling with gratitude. "Your support means the world to me."

"Hey," I suggested, feeling the need for relaxation and celebration. "Why don't we stay in tonight? We can order some Chinese food delivery, watch one of those sappy movies you saw on the app, and *enjoy* each other's company."

I wiggled my eyebrows while giving her a silly grin when I said *enjoy*. She laughed, knowing full well that when I said enjoy, I meant to spend a good portion of my time between her thighs.

"Sounds perfect to me," Aurora agreed, biting her bottom lip. Her shirt slipped a bit more off her shoulder, exposing that yummy skin.

Oh yeah, I planned on enjoying her a few times today.

As we settled onto the couch, duck sauce smears on astrophysics journal pages serving as coasters, the glow of the television screen casting a soft light across the room. Aurora leaned into me, resting her head on my shoulder as we laughed together at the antics of the characters on screen. It was a simple moment, but it felt like everything I had ever wanted, right here in this apartment.

We spent hours wrapped up in each other's arms, losing ourselves in the stories unfolding before us. The outside world, with its expectations and pressures, faded away as we found solace in one another.

When she shifted across my lap seeking popcorn my erection pressed against her, it was less than five minutes before she was sucking that dick down her throat.

And when she was leaning over the counter trying to figure out what we should stream next, that juicy ass peaking out the bottom of that shirt, I was so happy to find out she'd forgone the panties.

Yes, I enjoyed her a few times as we chilled.

As the evening drew to a close and the credits rolled on the last movie, I glanced at Aurora, her face illuminated by the flickering light from the TV. Her eyes met mine, and I could see the happiness that filled her, the excitement for the future she was about to embark on—and I knew that, no matter what challenges we faced, we would face them together.

"Langston, thank you for everything," she whispered, her voice barely audible above the sound of the movie's closing song. "I couldn't have come this far without you."

"You never have to thank me for loving you, Aurora," I replied, pulling her closer. "You've brought so much joy and inspiration into my life. I'll always be here for you."

She blinked up at me, and I realized a moment later that I'd said that I loved her. It flew out my mouth so naturally that it didn't faze me. And once I realized what I said, I just wanted to say it again.

But before I could, she cupped my face softly and pulled me in for a deep kiss I thought would last forever.

When she pulled away, I saw that she'd begun to cry.

"I love you too," she whispered. I wrapped my arms around her, wondering how I'd managed to meet the other half of my soul.

It was a simple day, but one that etched into my memory. And all I could want was more simple Sundays like this.

Aurora

The glow of the television illuminated Langston's face, casting a warm light on his handsome features. As I watched him, I couldn't help but think about how far I'd come since arriving back in Chicago.

My life had been a whirlwind of change, yet Langston had remained a constant source of support.

His hand rested on my hip as we lay tangled together on the couch, his fingertips humming against my skin like live wires. I surrounded by a shield against every ghost from my past.

The rain outside continued to fall, creating a cozy cocoon around us as we shared our dreams, fears, and hopes for the future.

"Maria has been amazing so far," I shared with Langston, my voice filled with excitement. "She's already shown the video of me singing to you at Aunt Cecily's to some producers, and one of them, the one who's worked on some of my favorite albums, is interested in a possible project."

Langston's eyes lit up as he heard the news. "That's incredible, Aurora! I'm so proud of you for taking control of your career and making these decisions for yourself."

"Thank you," I replied. "I couldn't have done it without your support and encouragement. Cutting Marcus out of my life was difficult, but it's allowed me to... I don't know, be *me*, I guess."

His embrace hardened protectively. "Marcus never deserved you."

As one of the movies ended, I felt a pull of emotion. I looked up into the face that filled so much of my heart. "Langston, thank you for everything. I couldn't have come this far without you."

He pulled me closer and stared down "You never have to thank me for loving you, Aurora. You've brought so much joy and inspiration into my life. I'll always be here for you."

All I could do was blink when the phrase *'loving you'* slipped from his lips. I felt it, but *had he said it?* Marcus had never, ever said it. He looked as shocked as I did and was struggling to speak further, a look of confusion in his eyes.

But before he could try to play it down, I took that beautiful face in my hands and drew him in for a kiss. As his lips touched mine, a sob caught in my throat, and a moment later I had tears streaming down my cheeks.

I didn't realize until this moment how much I longed to be loved and to love openly in return.

"I love you too," I whispered. I wrapped my arms around him, wondering how I'd managed to meet the other half of my soul.

He wrapped his arms around me in return, and I felt whole.

"Here's to new beginnings," Langston whispered, kissing my temple. And as I closed my eyes, basking in the warmth of his embrace and the promise of a brighter future, I couldn't help but agree.

A few days had passed since that Sunday evening. I had signed with Maria first thing on Monday. The news of her divorce from Tony, as well as my signing, was now public. Sitting on the couch in Langston's apartment with my phone in hand, I scrolled through social media, reading the comments and speculations about the situation.

"Maria divorcing Tony and signing that Aurora chick? Seems like Marcus is really losing it all," read one comment. Another said, *"I bet Marcus is the cause of all these relationship issues. Good for Aurora to get away from him!"* Many people seemed to point fingers at Marcus, blaming him for both the professional and personal turmoil surrounding him.

"Langston, did you see this?" I asked, showing him some of the comments online. He was working on the couch next to me, deep in thought in what looked like a star map. He stopped what he was doing and looked at the screen and let out a low whistle.

"Wow, babe, the news is spreading like wildfire. It's like a media frenzy out there," he said, shaking his head. "But don't worry about what they're saying. You know the truth, and that's what matters."

I nodded, realizing that despite the gossip and speculation, I had done the right thing by distancing myself from Marcus and aligning with Maria. The industry buzz generated by the news only served to fuel my determination to succeed and prove myself as an artist.

As days turned into weeks, the chatter around Maria's divorce and my signing began to die down, but the excitement within the music industry remained. Producers and other artists were beginning to take notice of me, expressing interest in collaborations and potential projects. It seems they finally looked at old footage and realized I was always there in the background queuing the band, giving my best to backup vocals, and cheering for who was then "my man."

Now it looked like it was my turn.

With each passing day, I grew more confident in myself – not just as an artist, but as a woman. And as I continued to grow and evolve, so too did my relationship with Langston. We shared intimate and tender moments together, our physical connection reflecting the depth of our emotional bond.

I was inspired, penning new music that reflected my newfound strength, and my budding experience of true love. And I was actually excited to share the new music bubbling from my soul.

"Here's to us," I whispered one night as we lay entwined beneath the sheets, our hearts beating in sync with one another. "To our future – and all its possibilities.

"Here's to us," Langston echoed, his voice soft but steady. His warm breath caressed my skin, and a shiver of delight ran down my spine.

"Langston," I said, raising my head to meet his gaze. "I know we've been through a lot in a short time, but I truly believe we're stronger because of it. And I'm so grateful for you. Most men would run from this messy situation I'm in. "

He smiled warmly. "Aurora, it's OK. None of this is on you." He let out a deep sigh of frustration. "On God, this is all on that dude. But he ain't gonna get in between something the stars aligned."

Our gazes locked and slowly, we moved closer to one another, our lips meeting in a gentle, tender kiss that seemed to encompass all the love and passion we shared.

As our bodies pressed closer together, the warmth we created was more than just physical – it was like my soul was on fire. Our hands roamed over each other's skin, exploring what had become familiar curves and contours while discovering new depths of pleasure.

I wanted to tell him more. I wanted to tell him I agreed with the cosmic alignment of our bond. But I couldn't speak, as his growl vibrated low against my neck, a primal counterpoint to his hands mapping my hips like territory he'd claimed long before tonight. I knew that was the end of our conversation.

Chapter 13

Aurora

My fingers trembled as I scrolled through the vicious comments and insults Marcus posted about me on every social media platform. Each word stabbed deeper, twisting the knife he'd buried long ago. How could he be so cruel? We were together for years, and now he acted as if I never meant anything to him.

I took a deep breath and closed my eyes, trying to steady my nerves. I kept telling myself that his words held no power over me. I wouldn't give him the satisfaction of knowing how much he hurt me.

Among all his posts was one that said "Headed To Chicago #Truth-Time." Marcus was going to do a radio interview to address the rumors. And of course, being the bastard he was, he decided to spew his lies in the city I'd come to find solace in.

A soft knock rattled my bedroom door. "Aurora? It's time."

I opened my eyes and stood, smoothing the wrinkles from my dress. When I emerged, Aunt Cecily grasped my hands in hers. "You're stronger than his lies. Don't forget that."

I managed a weak smile. "I know. It's just hard--"

"Seeing the man you once loved become the villain? But you have people," her eyes softened, and she tucked a stray curl behind my ear, "who love and know you for the wonderful person you are."

Arm in arm, we went next door to join Langston and Malcolm in the studio. They turned as we entered, faces etched with concern. I waved them off before they could ask how I was doing. The less said about Marcus, the better.

The radio interview had already started. Malcolm connected his phone to a Bluetooth speaker. We gathered around, and with a punched button on an app, Marcus' voice flooded the room.

"Thanks for having me on the show. I have some things I want to clear up about my break up with Aurora Knight..."

His smug tone made my stomach churn. I had opted to listen instead of watching the interview streamed. I could still imagine his frame sprawled out in the studio, all too comfortable with his lies. I gripped the edge of the console. Beside me, Langston tensed, jaw clenched.

Marcus droned on about our "passionate relationship" and how I had "blindsided" him with our breakup. Lies. All lies. He spun a tale of romance and heartbreak to make himself seem the victim, never once mentioning his cruelty or manipulation.

My hands curled into fists. How dare he. After everything he put me through, he had the audacity to drag my name through the mud to salvage his reputation.

"...and then, I found out she was involved with another man," Marcus's voice oozed insincerity. "This guy, let me tell you, he's a real piece of work. Thinks he's too good for his own community because he's got a fancy degree and some letters behind his name."

Langston's hand balled into a fist, and Aunt Cecily placed a soothing touch on his arm. Marcus's words were like poison, seeping into the cracks of my already fragile state. He continued, his voice dripping with mock sorrow.

"Seems like he's spent so much time looking at the stars, he's forgotten where he comes from. Can't respect a guy like that. And Aurora, well, she got wrapped up in his world, left her roots behind too. She singing about stars and crap, forgetting that she was with one."

I could barely breathe. His syllabic venom found its mark, exactly as Marcus intended. It was a calculated attack, designed to hit where it hurt most—our identities, our sense of belonging. Marcus knew exactly what he was doing, and it was working.

"Must be hard, pretending to be something you're not," Marcus went on, audacity lacing his tone. "But hey, maybe they're perfect for each other, both lost in their little fantasy worlds. Her pretending she's a musician. Him pretending he's black, he's one of *us*."

I sensed Aunt Cecily's gaze on me, assessing the damage. "Don't listen to him, Aurora," she said. "He's just trying to bring you down to his level."

But how could I not listen? Marcus's words echoed in my mind, a relentless reminder of how vulnerable we were to his twisted narratives. He had done his research, knew which buttons to press, and wasn't afraid to push them. My heart ached for Langston, who had always struggled with fitting in, only to have someone like Marcus ridicule his achievements and twist them into something ugly.

I numbly nodded. Marcus had declared war, and it was clear he didn't care who he hurt in the process.

Tony's voice crackled through the speakers, a venomous drawl that sent a chill down my spine. I didn't realize he was there since we were listening instead of watching. "And let's not forget about Maria," he began, and I could almost hear the smirk in his voice. "Bisexual and wild, that one. Did you know she and Aurora had a little... rendezvous? Oh yeah, it wasn't just about the music."

My hands clenched into fists at my sides as Tony painted a sordid picture for all of Chicago, all of the world, to lap up. He didn't stop there. "Aurora, she's always been ambitious, willing to do whatever—or whoever—it takes to get ahead in this industry."

A collective gasp filled Aunt Cecily's cozy studio, but I barely registered it. The room seemed to spin, my head throbbing with each word.

"Langston..." Malcolm's voice was cautious, laced with concern.

But Langston's face had gone from hurt to livid in an instant, the veins corded at his temples like barbed wire beneath skin. "That's a damned lie!" he exploded, his voice thick with fury. Langston didn't even know me back then, but even he knew immediately that it was a lie. His tall frame shook with barely restrained anger, his dark eyes aflame. "Marcus is going to pay for this!"

"Easy, man," Malcolm tried again, placing a steadying hand on Langston's shoulder. But it was like trying to calm a tempest with a whisper; Langston was beyond hearing, beyond reason.

"Talking about me is one thing," Langston spat out the words, "but dragging Aurora and other people through the mud like that? Accusing her of...of..." He couldn't even say it, the taste of the words too vile to cross his lips.

"Langston," I reached out, my own voice faint, my heart splintering for him. "Please, don't let them get to you. They're not worth it."

But he was already pacing, a tethered stallion thrashing against reins. Marcus's voice still filled the background as he spun false histories. Every disparaging remark about his identity, every insinuation that he was less than, that he hated his own, added fuel to Langston's inner fire. Marcus had struck a nerve, deep and raw, questioning Langston's authenticity, his place in the world he loved and fought so hard to uplift.

"Promiscuous?" Langston turned sharply to face me, the word bitter on his tongue. "He has no right. None! Aurora, you are the furthest thing from what they're painting you to be."

Aunt Cecily was at his side now, her presence a sturdy comfort. "Langston, breathe," she soothed, her voice a balm amidst the chaos. "Rumor's like this are normal in the world Marcus is from. This is exactly what they want—a reaction, a spectacle."

But Langston wasn't from Marcus' world, and it was clear that Aunt Cecily's words hadn't cooled him. As the interview continued to play, Marcus's laughter a taunting echo as he talked about all his plans to have fun in Chicago, my safe haven. The angry lines in Langston's face hardened.

"Something has to be done," he muttered, his voice low but determined. "They can't get away with this. Not this time. Imma have a *talk* with him."

And though he stood still, I knew Langston was already miles away, plotting a course of action that probably was a bad idea.

"*Talk* to Marcus?" I echoed, my voice laced with trepidation. "Langston, that's exactly what he wants."

"Maybe so," Langston said, his eyes flaring with a resolve I both admired and feared. "But I can't sit here and let him drag our names through the mud. Not without confronting him."

"Let me come with you," Malcolm offered, standing up. The studio was suddenly too small, Aunt Cecily's trinkets and sculptures witnesses to the tension that vibrated through the room.

"Please, be careful," I pleaded, reaching out to touch Langston's arm in a futile attempt to tether him to reason. But his muscles were taut beneath my fingers, coiled and ready for action.

"Stay here, Aurora. I'll handle it," Langston assured, but there was a storm brewing behind his calm facade. With a look that spelled trouble, he stormed out, Malcolm on his heels like a silent guardian. The door slam reverberated through my bones

The door slammed shut, leaving a void where Langston had stood.

Aunt Cecily sighed deeply, her hands finding their way to her hips as she turned to me. Her silver hair seemed to catch the light from the windows, creating a halo around her wise features. "That boy has the weight of the world on his shoulders," she murmured.

"Marcus is relentless," I admitted, anger seeping into my words. "How can one person be so cruel?"

"Power and fear," Aunt Cecily said simply. "He feels his influence slipping and is scared. But Aurora, darling, remember your truth. You are not the lies he spreads."

"Truth seems to have little power against his influence," I said bitterly.

"Then maybe it's time to fight fire with a blaze of your own," Aunt Cecily suggested, her gaze sharp and challenging. "You might consider breaking that non-confidentiality agreement. The world should see Marcus for who he really is."

"Wouldn't that just make things worse?" I asked, though part of me itched to reveal every dark corner of Marcus's being. What if no one believed me? What if I sounded like another "bitter black woman"? Then I'd risk being sued and still not get the results I wanted.

"Sometimes, child, the only way out is through," she replied with a serene confidence that somehow eased the turmoil within me. "And you, Aurora, are a force all your own. It's time he learned that."

Langston

The city blurred past the window of Malcolm's car, but I couldn't see it. My vision swam with crimson static, my mind replaying Marcus's words on loop. The audacity of him to spew such lies about Aurora, and to drag me into his filthy narrative—it boiled my blood.

"Man, we can't roll up there and start swinging," Malcolm said, his voice a mixture of concern and calm. He'd always been the one to temper my impulses with reason.

"Marcus needs to be put in check," I growled, my fingers curling into fists involuntarily.

"Look, I get it. The guy's a first-class jerk. But you're not just some guy from the block anymore. You've got students looking up to you, papers to publish, awards to win. Getting into a scrap and ending up a headline isn't worth it."

"Since when did you become the voice of caution?" I shot back, though part of me knew he was right.

"Since my boy became too important to throw it away on some egotistical singer who ain't worth the time," Malcolm replied, shooting me a look that was all seriousness.

I sighed, leaning my head back against the seat. Anger was still coursing through me, but Malcolm's words were starting to penetrate the fog of rage. We were nearing the venue where Marcus had announced he'd be making an appearance after the interview. The thought of seeing his smug face in person made my hands itch with the desire to make contact.

"Alright, so we don't fight him," I conceded. "But I'm not just going to sit back and let him slander us. We need to do something."

Malcolm exhaled through his nose. "Let's case it first. No rash moves, okay?" He parked the car a block away from our destination.

"Okay," I agreed, but my resolve to stay calm was brittle as telescope glass under pressure. As we walked toward the venue, my thoughts churned. There had to be a way to expose Marcus for the liar he was, a method to strip him of his power without sinking to his level.

"Remember who you are, Langston," Malcolm said quietly as we approached the growing crowd outside the venue. His reminder was a lifeline thrown into the tumultuous sea of my emotions.

I am Langston Wilkerson, an astrophysics professor, a man of intellect and reason. Not a pawn in Marcus James' twisted game. With every step, I repeated the mantra in my head, determined to confront Marcus with dignity, if confrontation was unavoidable. *I am Professor Langston Wilkerson, an astrophysics professor, a man of intellect and reason.*

"Let's see what he has to say for himself," I muttered as we merged into the throng of people, all here to witness the spectacle that Marcus James had become.

"Hey," Malcolm said, placing a hand on my shoulder as we stood among the crowd. "I know you're pissed, and trust me, I am too. But getting into a physical or public confrontation isn't going to help anyone. You're a professional, Langston. Don't let this guy ruin your career."

He was right, of course. If I acted foolishly now, I would be playing right into Marcus' hands, giving him the attention he craved and lending credence to his negative tirades about Aurora and me. It wasn't worth it.

"Okay. Let's head back," I agreed reluctantly, anger still simmering beneath the surface. As we turned to leave, Malcolm's next words caught my attention.

"Wouldn't it be nice if some dirt about Marcus came to light?" he mused. "Something that wouldn't blow back on us or Aurora..."

An idea sparked in my mind, like a star igniting in the vast cosmos. I didn't go into detail, but the concept took root, growing stronger with each passing moment.

"Let's get out of here," I suggested, tugging at Malcolm's arm. "I've got an idea, but we need to regroup first. I think we can make Marcus regret messing with us – without sinking to his level."

Hopeful glances were exchanged as we made our way back to the car before we were spotted. I'm sure at least one person would have recognized the #SexyScientist, which would actually go against the plan forming in my mind.

The air in Malcolm's basement was thick with the ozone tang of running servers and mildew, an ambiance that both of us found oddly comforting. It was a makeshift recording studio and gaming room that bore witness to many of our shared dreams and hidden fears. Now, it served as our war room, a place where strategy overcame raw emotion.

Hunched over Malcolm's desktop, my fingers danced across the keys, crafting words like equations meant to balance out the injustice. I was on a social media platform famed for its anonymity. It didn't have advertisements to get people to join, and you had to navigate to it directly. It wasn't a social media site that the masses frequented. It wasn't flashy, full of pictures and videos. It was mostly streams of text conversations and information that disappeared forever as quickly as it posted.

Here, conversations were whispers in the wind, gone before anyone could grasp them firmly. Once posted, they stayed visible for a short time, allowing back-and-forth conversations between anonymous users.

It was a site only few, and certain kind of people, knew about. The kind of people I knew. The kind of people who were about to get to know Marcus real well.

"Read this out loud?" I asked, gesturing towards the screen without taking my eyes off it.

"Sure," Malcolm agreed, leaning over my shoulder to see better. "*Isn't it curious how some folks feel entitled to belittle black male academics? Claiming they're neither real men nor black enough. Just because someone's path isn't strewn with clichés doesn't make it less valid. Maybe it's time an example is made out of people like MJ.*" Malcolm whistled low – three rising notes. "Dem's fightin' words."

"I'ma post it," I said after a moment's hesitation, my index finger hovering above the 'Enter' key before pressing down decisively.

Almost immediately, responses began to populate beneath the post. Handles like @SchrödingerTroll420 and @HexCodeQueen blinked into existence. The users were shrouded in digital anonymity, yet some seemed to resonate with my sentiment more personally than others.

"*Brother speaks truth,*" one user wrote, "*People like MJ are the real problem.*"

"*I heard that shit. We all know who he was talking about. Professor W's work inspires us all,*" another added, a nod to my identity without outright exposing me. "*We need more minds like his, not less.*"

I read each comment, feeling the solidarity of a marginalized slice of my own community. They understood the struggle to feel a part of what they were born into. Their words were fuel, igniting a sense of purpose within me. It wasn't just about Aurora anymore; it was about standing up against a culture that tended to demean those who dared to be different.

"Looks like you've got quite the fanbase," Malcolm chuckled, impressed by the outpouring of support.

"Let's hope they're more than just fans," I replied, voice laced with determination. "Let's see if they code justice better than rage."

As we sat there in the dim light of the basement, surrounded by the hum of Malcolm's equipment, I thought of my own journey – from the streets of Chicago to the academia's ivory towers. My pursuit of the stars had always been a solitary one, but now, faced with a galaxy of supporters, I realized that perhaps I wasn't so alone after all.

Malcolm leaned back in his chair, the leather's creak punctuating the silence that had settled between us. He watched as my fingers flew across the keyboard, responding with careful precision to each new message that popped up on the screen. The legion of self-proclaimed nerds was rallying, their digital avatars buzzing.

"Marcus has no idea," Malcolm said, a hint of admiration coloring his tone. "He's poked the bear one too many times."

"More like a swarm of bees," I corrected quietly, eyes never leaving the screen. "And they're all buzzing for justice."

The words were barely out when the virtual space erupted into a flurry of activity. Anonymous profiles with handles like 'QuantumHack' and 'CyberSleuth42' began sharing intricate plans—coded messages, hidden IPs, and layers of encryption. Someone with the username 'PixelPunisher' mentioned having access to high-end video editing software, offering to splice together incriminating footage of Marcus with the finesse of a Hollywood producer.

"Damn, these guys are serious," Malcolm muttered under his breath, both impressed and slightly intimidated by the sheer level of expertise being casually thrown around.

"Skill is mightier than muscle," I replied, paraphrasing an old proverb. My heart raced at the thought of what this digital army could achieve—a public reckoning without throwing a single punch.

As more users chimed in, pledging their unique abilities to the cause, the threads of a plan weaved together. Hackers talked of accessing Marcus' social media accounts, exposing his hypocrisy. Surveillance wizards discussed tracking his movements, ensuring he couldn't escape the truth. And there were those who specialized in information gathering, promising to unearth every sordid detail of Marcus' past. And I knew that Marcus had plenty of things he wouldn't want the public to know.

"Marcus doesn't stand a chance against this kind of firepower," Malcolm observed, shaking his head in disbelief. "These aren't just nerds; they're warriors of the information age."

I nodded, a small smile playing on my lips. "Marcus hacked reality once. Time we rootkit his ego."

It wasn't just about embarrassing Marcus anymore—it was about reclaiming my own narrative and Aurora's. As the voices online multiplied, each one echoing my call to action, I knew they were crafting something powerful, something transformative.

Just as I was about to respond to another message, a video call notification popped up on the screen. I recognized the caller ID, and my face lit up in surprise.

"Hey, it's our favorite spook!" Malcolm exclaimed, grinning from ear to ear.

Craig was a friend we played DnD with virtually a few times a month.

"Speak of the devil," I said as I accepted the call. The screen flickered to life, revealing Craig's familiar face. He worked for a US government agency as an analyst, and despite the secretive nature of his job, he had a warm and charismatic presence that put everyone at ease.

"Langston! Malcolm! How are my two favorite troublemakers?" our friend greeted us, his voice light and jovial, belying the fact that he was calling from his high-security office.

"We're good, man. Better now that you've joined our little party," Malcolm replied, clapping me on the back.

"Speaking of parties," Craig began, his eyes narrowing teasingly, "I see you've been stirring up quite a storm online."

I hesitated, unsure of how much our friend knew. "What do you mean?"

"Come on, Langston," Craig laughed. "You think I wouldn't recognize your handiwork? I am an expert, after all." He winked conspiratorially. "Plus, with Marcus' interview going viral, it wasn't hard to put two and two together."

"Alright, you caught me," I admitted sheepishly, though I couldn't help but have a sense of pride at having sparked such a powerful movement. "But what can I say? Marcus needed to be taken down a peg or two."

"More like ten pegs," Malcolm chimed in, smirking. "He's messed with the wrong people this time."

Our friend nodded, a determined glint in his eye. "Well, count me in. I want to help you make sure Marcus never bothers you or Aurora again."

"Are you sure?" I asked, touched by Craig's loyalty but worried about the potential risks involved. "I don't want you getting into trouble because of us."

"Trust me," he replied, a grin spreading across his face. "I've got this. Just leave it to me and my... unique skill set. Just remember to name you and that fine Aurora's firstborn son after me."

As the call ended, I couldn't help but feel a mixture of relief and trepidation. I knew that with our friend's help, we had more than a fighting chance against Marcus. But I also understood that the stakes were higher than ever before.

Aurora

I paced the living room floor. Hours had passed since I last heard from Langston, and I was uneasy. Aunt Cecily watched me with concern, her brow furrowed.

"Sweetheart, I know you're worried about Langston, but I'm sure he's fine," she said softly, trying to reassure me. "He's a smart man, and he can take care of himself."

"I know, but what if--" My thoughts scattered as Aunt Cecily stood abruptly.

"Enough of this. You cannot let Marcus continue to control your life like this. It's time for you to face him, once and for all."

"Are you sure?" I asked, hesitant to take on such a challenge. But deep down, I knew she was right. I needed to regain control of my life and career, even if it meant breaking the non-confidentiality agreement and exposing Marcus for who he really was.

"Absolutely," Aunt Cecily said, her eyes filled with determination. She went to pick up her purse. "Now, let's go find that snake and put an end to his venomous games."

Together, we left the house and headed to the evening public appearance Marcus mentioned during the radio interview. Some new club downtown he apparently was buying into. The knot in my stomach tightened as we approached the venue, but I squared my shoulders and steeled myself for the confrontation ahead.

The sky had turned a dusky purple, the city's lights painting shadows on our faces as Aunt Cecily and I walked in silence. Each step like moving through molasses, my heart pounding against my ribs with a mix of fear and determination. Several hours had passed since Langston stormed out, his phone now going straight to voicemail. The eerie silence from him was unnerving, but Aunt Cecily's resolve was infectious.

"Remember, Aurora," she said, her voice steady, "you have every right to stand up for yourself. That confidentiality agreement isn't worth your peace of mind. And I'm here with you."

I cast a look over at her. My aunt was small, and fashionably classy. But in case people forgot, she was South Side-born—polished pearls over steel. The look on her face said she was ready to give Marcus and anyone else that stepped to us a taste.

I nodded, taking a deep breath. Confronting Marcus was no small feat, but the thought of cowering under his shadow for any longer fueled my courage. I wouldn't – couldn't – let his lies and manipulation dictate my future anymore. It was time to reclaim my story.

"Let's get this done," I said with newfound conviction, and together we approached the velvet ropes where Marcus had promised the public he'd be.

The venue was buzzing with activity, people milling around, their voices blending into a cacophony of excitement and anticipation. As we got closer, the thumping bass from inside reverberated in my chest.

As we neared the door, the bouncer eyed us, a clipboard in hand. But Aunt Cecily gave him a look that seemed to say, 'Try and stop us.' Maybe it was her look, or maybe he recognized me as the woman everyone was gossiping about, but the bouncer stepped aside without so much as a word. Inside, the club's lights and the pulsating music created an almost surreal atmosphere. Marcus's presence loomed over the room like a dark cloud even before I saw him.

The moment we laid eyes on Marcus, my pulse roared like storm surge. He was there, standing with Tony, their heads close together, speaking in hushed tones that didn't match the bravado he'd spewed on air. They were behind another velvet rope, separated from the crowd..

"Miss, you can't go any further," a mountain of a man stepped in front of us, his arms folded across a broad chest.

"Can't I?" Aunt Cecily's voice was deceptively sweet, her silver hair shimmering under the club's kaleidoscope lights. "My dear, I've walked through doors that would make your knees buckle. Now, are you going to stop me from having a word with that pitiful excuse of a man?"

The bodyguard's face twitched, a hint of a smile betraying his stoic facade. "Ma'am, I'm just doing my job."

"And I'm doing mine," she countered, leaning closer to him. "I assure you, it's far scarier than yours. Now, step aside."

It might have been the steel in her gaze or the way she held herself like royalty, but the bodyguard hesitated only a moment longer before stepping to the side, mumbling a gruff, "Make it quick."

"Thank you kindly," Aunt Cecily said, patting his arm. We moved past him, pushing through the last barrier between us and our confrontation.

"Marcus!" My voice carried over the music, strong and clear, slicing through the revelry like a bolt of lightning. Heads turned, whispers began to spread like wildfire. Marcus turned to face me, his expression a mix of surprise and annoyance.

"Here to beg for forgiveness?" His tone dripped with condescension, an attempt to belittle me in front of the onlookers.

"Forgiveness?" The word tasted bitter on my tongue. "No, Marcus. I'm not here to grovel at your feet. I'm here to tell you, in front of all these witnesses, that your words, your lies, they no longer hold power over me."

Tony tried to interject, to weave some sly comment into the fray, but I held up my hand, silencing him. "And whatever fiction you've concocted about my relationship with Langston, let me be perfectly clear—it's none of your business. Our love, our bond, is something you could never understand."

Marcus's face hardened, the lines of his jaw clenching as he struggled to maintain his poised exterior. But I could see the cracks forming, the uncertainty flickering in his cold eyes.

"Your attempts to smear me, to tarnish my image, they end today," I continued, sensing the weight of every eye upon us. "I am not your victim, Marcus. I am Aurora—singer, artist, survivor. And I will not be broken by the likes of you."

Aunt Cecily stood beside me, her presence a pillar of support. A muscle twitched in Marcus's jaw—the first crack in his polished sneer. He was always a bit afraid of my aunt who never really liked him. His mouth opening and closing like a fish out of water.

"Your little manager there," Aunt Cecily's voice cut through the tension, pointing a slender finger at Tony with an air of accusation so sharp it could slice through steel, "seems to have forgotten the company he keeps. Isn't that right, Tony? Or should I say... Marcus's secret partner in more than just music?"

Tony's eyes widened, his lips parted but no sound came out. His gaze flickered to Marcus, then back to Aunt Cecily, as if weighing his options.

"See, children," Aunt Cecily continued, her voice tinged with a mocking sweetness, "it takes more than a handsome face and a silver tongue to navigate this world. It takes integrity—something you both are sorely lacking."

The crowd murmured, phones held up high to capture every moment, every word. They were thirsty for the truth, and Aunt Cecily was serving it on a platter.

"Enough of this," Marcus snapped, his composure cracking like thin ice underfoot. "Who do you think you are, Aurora? You come into my club with this disrespect? After everything, you're still nothing—a nobody trying to ride on my wave of success!"

His words were venomous, meant to wound, but they bounced off me like pebbles against armor.

"Actually," a voice called from the crowd, strong and clear, "she's everything you're not, Marcus. Honest, talented, and actually liked."

"Have you seen the video?" another chimed in, pressing forward. "It shows exactly who Marcus really is."

Marcus's expression flushed as he searched the faces in the crowd for the source of the dissent. But it didn't matter who had spoken; the truth was out, and the tide was turning.

"Whatever," he spat out. "Anyone that believes that is a stupid as this bitch."

But even as he said it, he shrank before us like paper curling in flame.

A woman standing close by handed me her phone, the screen displaying a video clip that made my heart race. Marcus and Tony were caught in a passionate embrace, their lips locked together hungrily. As the video continued, Marcus' mouth was moving, and someone had added closed captions. I read the words that showed Marcus speaking ill of me, as if I were nothing more than an irritating distraction in his life.

"Look at this one too," a man nearby said, showing me another clip on his phone. It was me during band practice, also captioned. It showed me instructing the musicians on how to play the song I had clearly written, encouraging the musicians to put their own spin on it. Meanwhile, Marcus sat off idly in the background of the video, lazily telling everyone to just follow my lead since he didn't know the song yet and couldn't be bothered to care.

"See?" the woman said, meeting my gaze. "You're the real talent here."

Marcus's eyes widened as someone closer showed him the incriminating footage, his face contorted with rage. He turned to me, his fury barely contained. "You set this up, didn't you? You couldn't stand that I was moving on, so you had to drag me down too!"

"Are you seriously accusing me of this?" I asked incredulously. "I had no idea these videos even existed until now!"

His anger escalating, Marcus raised his hand—but Langston materialized behind him, grabbing Marcus's wrist in a vice-like grip. With a swift, powerful punch, Langston sent Marcus crashing to the ground.

"Get away from her," Langston growled, his protective instincts on full display. He stood huffing over Marcus. When he dared to try to get up again, a powerful hook from Langston sent him sprawling.

Malcolm appeared as well, stepping between Langston and Tony, who seemed ready to jump into the fray. But Malcolm's hulking presence alone was enough to halt any further aggression. The bodyguard who had let them all in didn't move a muscle to help.

"Stand down," Malcolm warned, his voice firm and steady. "This is over."

As the tension reached its peak, it became apparent that every second of this confrontation had been captured on camera by the eager crowd. The truth was out there for all to see.

With a final, defiant glance at Marcus and Tony, Langston took my hand, leading me away from the chaos that had unfolded. Aunt Cecily and Malcolm followed closely behind, forming a protective barrier around us.

In that moment, I knew that I had finally taken control of my own narrative and stepped into the light as the strong, independent woman I was meant to be. There was no way this could be skewed to make Marcus look like anything other than what he was--a complete ass.

Chapter 14

Aurora

The city lights blurred past the car window, mere streaks of neon against the velvet night as Malcolm navigated through the quiet streets. The hum of the engine was a soothing bassline to the symphony of my still-racing heart. We'd left Aunt Cecily's comforting aura behind, her house another shadow swallowed by the darkness as we drove away. Now, it was just Langston, Malcolm, and me—my protectors in this surreal aftermath.

I leaned back in the passenger seat, my mind replaying the night's confrontation over a looped beat. I had faced Marcus, my voice not just audible but commanding. And Langston... didn't condone violence, but watching my man lay out Marcus had my yoni throbbing. Having a man stand up for me was sexy. It was as if his fist carried all the hurt and frustration that Marcus had orchestrated in my life. My chest swelled with an unfamiliar pride, a sense of accomplishment that was both sweet and fierce.

Langston's profile was calm, composed as he sat beside me. His athletic frame relaxed into the leather seat, a stark contrast to the tension that had tightened every muscle when his fist connected with Marcus. Underneath his urban-cool attire, the faint outline of his NASA-themed T-shirt peeked out with a thick gold chain adorning his neckline, a silent reminder of the galaxy of complexities that made up the man he was.

"Can you believe it?" I murmured, barely above a whisper, the words more for myself than for them. "We actually stood up to him—to Marcus."

Langston's dark eyes flickered toward me. He didn't need to speak; his actions at the club had already said everything. Still, the warmth of his gaze wrapped around me like an anchor line.

"Hey," Malcolm called from the driver's seat, his locs dancing with each turn of his head, his tone light but laced with pride. "You were amazing back there, Aurora. A true star."

"Thank you." The gratitude in my voice was genuine, but it was also more than that—it was a recognition of the journey I had embarked on since walking away from Marcus, since finding refuge with Aunt Cecily, and since allowing Langston to become an unexpected beacon in my storm.

"Langston," I said, turning my full attention to him, "I can't thank you enough for coming to help me. You've been there for me every step of the way." My voice hitched with emotion, and I reached for his hand, intertwining our fingers together.

"Always." His thumb brushed my knuckles, voice gravel-rough. "You don't have to face anything alone anymore."

"Did you see those videos people were showing me?" I asked, remembering the footage that had surfaced, providing undeniable evidence of Marcus and Tony's affair, as well as Marcus' blatant disrespect toward me and my contributions to our music.

Langston nodded, his expression a mixture of anger and sympathy. "Yeah, I saw them. It's infuriating how they treated you. But now everyone knows the truth—that you're an incredibly talented artist who deserves recognition for her work."

Malcolm chimed in from the front seat, "That's right! Those videos only prove what we already knew—Aurora, you're *that* girl."

His infectious smile made me burst with laughter. The support from both Langston and Malcolm warmed my heart.

"Actually," Malcolm added, "those videos came to light thanks to Langston's legion of supporters."

I turned to Langston in surprise. "What does he mean?"

Langston shrugged. "I may have mentioned to a few people how upset I was about Marcus and Tony cutting you out of the album. And a few of those friends are kind of like me-"

"Nerds!" Malcolm said in his normally teasing manner. His word was met with a slap from Langston to the back of the head. Their antics just made me laugh more.

"Some of my *friends*," Langston continued, "took it upon themselves to dig up dirt on Marcus, and it looks like they found quite a bit."

"You did that for me?" I asked, blinking back tears of gratitude. The depths of Langston's love and devotion continued to astound me.

"Anything for you, Aurora," he replied earnestly.

"I've already seen posts proving Marcus cheated with other people too," Malcolm chimed in. "Langston's friends are good at what they do. Marcus is about to face a whole lot more than a few leaked videos."

Stunned, I shook my head in disbelief. "I had no idea. You didn't have to do any of this."

"We did," Langston insisted gently. "Because we care about you. We want to see Marcus and Tony get what they deserve for how they treated you."

I pulled Langston into a fierce hug, clinging to him as a fresh wave of emotion crashed over me. "What did I ever do to deserve friends like you?"

"You were just yourself, Aurora. And that's more than enough."

Langston's words settled in my bones, solid as a bassline.

Unable to resist any longer, I pulled Langston closer, and captured his lips in a searing kiss. Langston made a soft sound of surprise before returning the kiss with fervor.

We might have continued like that for some time if Malcolm hadn't cleared his throat pointedly from the driver's seat. "As touching as this is, do you mind waiting until you're behind closed doors?"

We broke apart, breathless and sheepish. Langston chuckled, a deep rumble in his chest that I felt more than heard. "My bad. You're right, we should continue this somewhere more private."

I smiled, smoothing the collar of his shirt. "Your place?"

Langston's eyes gleamed.

When Malcolm parked in front of the building, I pushed myself forward toward the front seat so I could look him in the face.

"Thank you, Malcolm, for everything," I said, leaning over to kiss his cheek.

He waved me off good-naturedly. "Don't mention it. You two have a good night now."

"We will," Langston promised with a devilish grin. He took my hand, lacing our fingers together and leading me from the car toward his building.

As soon as the door to the apartment closed behind us, Langston pressed me up against the wall and claimed my lips again.

"I've needed this," I whispered against his mouth.

"So have I," he said, his hand moving around my waist to untie the sash holding my wrap-around sweater closed. I slipped my arms out and let the garment fall open, revealing my body to him.

"Langston," I whimpered as his hot breath fanned over my neck.

He smiled against my skin and nipped at my earlobe, causing a shudder to run through me.

"You're so beautiful," he murmured, his voice rough with desire. He moved toward my breast and buried his face between them groaning before trailing light kisses downwards towards my stomach. He undid the clasp of the bra and let it fall too.

His rough hands cupped both my breasts gently before tracing circles around the dark brown nipples making them harden under his palm.

I leaned back into the sensation, letting him loosen the belt of my jeans before I shimmied them down. I stood before him in just my panties, panting, ready to be claimed by my protector. It seemed to make us both lose our minds for a moment. We tasted each other; our tongues tangling in a desperate dance that left me gasping for air.

I heard the soft sound of his zipper lowering, followed by his warm hand sliding up my thigh and between my legs. My breath hitched at the feel of his thumb rubbing against me through my panties.

"So wet for me," he whispered, his voice like a soft reverie.

I moaned into his mouth as he returned to claim my lips, unable to help myself, as he pushed my panties down and fingered me slowly, his other hand cupping a breast. I arched into his touch, needing more.

Langston's body trembled as he tasted me, his mouth seeking out every inch of my skin like he was starving for it. His cologne mixed with the scent of my arousal in the air and created an intoxicating blend. His thick erection pressed against me, showing how much he wanted me. As he carried me to his bedroom and laid me down on the soft sheets, I couldn't help but feel a surge of anticipation coursing through my veins.

His mouth traced a path down my chest, over my stomach, and lower, finally reaching the entrance to my palace. He pressed a possessive kiss there before trailing more of his warm saliva onto my skin, making me shiver with excitement. As he parted my legs, his gaze met mine, full of tenderness and dominance. He his teeth lightly graze against my inner thighs, causing goosebumps to rise on my skin. He licked me slowly, taking his time, and I couldn't help but grip the sheets tightly trying to rein in my demands for more.

His tongue flicked against my sensitive flesh, driving me wild with pleasure. Then, all of a sudden, he replaced his tongue with his fingers, circling my entrance before pushing one inside slowly. It was both achingly slow and unbearably erotic. I whimpered as he stretched me, filling me with more of his fingers until he was finally buried deep inside. His fingers thrust with a rhythm that matched the song that was starting to form in my mind.

Each thrust sent ripples of pleasure coursing through my body as I cried out his name. The sensation of being filled by him was unlike anything I'd ever experienced before. I came apart beneath him, screaming his praises as waves of pleasure washed over me. It was clear that Langston knew exactly what he was doing to me, and I couldn't help but love every single second of it.

As we both caught our breath, Langston slid his fingers out of me, leaving me aching for more. He moved up my body, pressing his hard length against my slick entrance. Without another word, sheathed himself in one smooth stroke, stretched me achingly full. He rolled his hips—a slow grind that melted into rhythmic thrusts—as our breaths tangled. It was all too much, but in the best possible way.

He grabbed my hips, holding me still as he took me harder and faster. The sound of skin slapping against skin echoed in the room, adding to the intense sensation. I felt him grow deeper inside me, his muscles flexing as he thrust into me with more force.

It was so orgasmic; it was musical, and I found myself literally singing his name in pleasure.

Just as I was about to explode, Langston slowed down, his thrusts becoming deeper and more powerful. The familiar tingles spread through my body, and then, all at once, he released me, sending me spiraling over the edge. I came with a force I didn't know was possible, my body shaking as wave after wave of pleasure washed over me.

I gripped onto his back, his muscles tight and slick with sweat. He began cursing, pushing harder, the slapping sound of our skin louder.

Langston followed me over the edge, groaning as he emptied himself inside me. We collapsed onto the bed together, our hearts pounding in unison.

Chapter 15

Aurora

The soft clink of silverware against china underscored our conversation—a far cry from the chaos that had defined my life weeks ago. Across from me sat Maria in the bistro we'd chosen for its privacy and quiet ambiance. There was a certain gravity to her demeanor, a sense of purpose that resonated with the part of me yearning for a fresh start.

"Take your time," Maria encouraged as I scanned the pages of the contract before me. "I want you to be comfortable with every clause, every commitment."

My fingers traced the lines of text, each word a stepping stone away from the person I was at the award ceremony—vulnerable, exposed—and towards who I could become under her guidance. The terms were clear and fair.

"Your vision," I hesitated under her steady gaze. "It's as if you ripped these dreams right out of my chest."

"Because I believe in you," she replied, her expression earnest. "I see an artist who is true to herself and her art. You're not just the first under my management, Aurora; you're the cornerstone of what I hope will be a legacy of authentic talent."

I allow myself a moment to bask in the warmth of potential success. A few weeks ago, I would have shied away from such praise, buried it under layers of self-doubt. But something within me was shifting, evolving.

"Authentic," I echoed softly, tasting the word. It felt like the salve to the wound left by betrayal. It was the essence of my music, the core of my being. And Maria saw that.

"Absolutely," she affirmed with a decisive nod. "We'll build your brand around that authenticity. People crave real emotion in their music, and you deliver that in spades."

We continued discussing logistics, creative direction, and marketing strategies—all the pieces of a puzzle that were slowly forming a picture of my future. As the evening waned, I found solace in the meticulous nature of our planning. In this world of contracts and careful considerations, there was no room for the chaos that once threatened to consume me.

"Thank you, Maria," I said, finally closing the folder and pushing it back across the table. "For believing in me when I had forgotten how to believe in myself."

"We are going to do amazing things together," she promised, raising her glass in a toast. "To new beginnings and chart-topping hits."

Our laughter mingled with the soft jazz playing in the background, and for the first time in a long while, my heart matched the rhythm of the music—a steady beat full of promise and anticipation.

We lingered over coffee, chatting casually about life and music and the latest celebrity gossip. It was good to laugh with another woman, to share the simple pleasures of friendship without an ulterior motive. Maria was becoming like the big sister I always wanted.

"Have you heard from Marcus?" she asked, after the waiter refilled my mug. "I know he's been trying to reach out since the incident at the club."

"Not directly." I frowned, thinking of the calls and texts I had ignored. "But I've seen the headlines. His new single isn't doing well, and Tony has been dropping clients left and right. Rumor has it, they're blaming each other for the failure."

Maria's eyes glinted with satisfaction. "Karma turns out to be exactly what Tony always said I was—a bitch. The music industry has a long memory, and what they did to you won't be easily forgotten."

"It's strange," I said slowly, "how things can change so quickly. A few months ago, Marcus and Tony were on top of the world, and I was struggling to pick up the pieces of my life. Now here we are, and our fortunes seem to have reversed."

"The universe has a way of balancing itself out in the end." Maria squeezed my hand gently. "You deserve every bit of success coming your way. Never forget that."

I smiled, blinking back the sting of tears. "I won't. And I'm ready to embrace the future, whatever it may bring."

Maria beamed, pride shining in her eyes. "That's my girl. The future is yours for the taking."

I laughed, shaking my head. "I still can't believe those leaked videos went viral. The timing couldn't have been more perfect. I know some unnamed sources are behind it—but where did the videos come from in the first place?"

"There was nothing accidental about it. Let's just say a little birdie slid into my DMs," Maria said, leaning closer. 'Asked if I had receipts on those bastards. I was all too happy to donate some incriminating footage of Marcus and Tony, anonymously, of course. I always keep receipts."

"You?" I stared at her in disbelief. "But how did you--?"

"Like I said, the universe has a way of balancing itself out." Her eyes gleamed with mischief. "And a little nudge to help the process along never hurts."

My throat tightened—part rage, part relief—as I grasped how far she'd gone for me. Maria had been intricate in the downfall of the two men who had caused me so much pain and betrayal. She had lifted me up at my lowest point, dusted me off, and helped set me back on the path towards my dreams.

I reached over and hugged her. "Thank you," I whispered. "For everything."

Maria hugged me back just as tightly. "You're welcome, girl. That's what friends are for."

We broke apart, and I wiped my eyes, laughing through the tears. "Look at me, crying in the middle of this restaurant. I must be quite the sight."

Maria thumbed away a tear below my lashes. "Smudged mascara suits you. War paint for the revolution. You ready to head out?"

I blushed, still overwhelmed by emotion and gratitude. "Yes, let's go."

The future was filled with possibilities, and Langston would be by my side every step of the way. Marcus and Tony were fading into the past, where they belonged, and a new chapter of my life was just beginning.

Maria waved to the waiter, signaling for the bill. As I composed myself, smoothing out the creases in my napkin, there was an air of mutual understanding between us—an unspoken acknowledgment that our bond had deepened beyond the realms of contracts and career strategies.

The waiter returned, and Maria settled the check with an assertive flick of her wrist. I admired her—she possessed a kind of self-assurance that I was only beginning to cultivate within myself.

Sunlight lashed the sidewalk. In the window's reflection, my face looked sharper—not brave, but hungry.

"I'll call you tomorrow," I said, gazing down the city street that stretched towards the community center where Langston awaited me. "Langston is part of an event across town, and I promised I'd be there."

"Of course," she replied, her eyes sparkling with shared enthusiasm. "You should be so proud of yourself, Aurora. Your career's taking off, and what you have found with that Langston... it's special."

"Thank you," I said softly, my thoughts drifting to the man who had rekindled the stars in my once-dim universe. "He's been my rock through all of this."

"Go to him, Aurora," Maria encouraged, gesturing with a nod toward the direction I needed to go. "Celebrate everything that's happening. This is your time."

With a smile that reflected the hope burgeoning within me, I turned on my heel, my steps light with anticipation. The sounds of the city hummed around me, and my heart raced, eager for the embrace of my beloved astrophysicist, and the joy of sharing every triumph, every challenge, side by side.

Langston would be waiting—no doubt fidgeting with his star-chart notes—but tonight, his steadiness was mine to claim.

Langston

The hum of the computer fans melded with the steady cadence of our conversation, creating a sort of technological symphony that underscored the importance of the moment. I was in my office with Jamal and Dr. Simone Davis, tied into a video conference with others to plan some aspects of the non-profit outreach.

An odd symmetry filled the room – mentor and mentee flanking me. Somehow I felt like all the attention was on me.

Jamal's eager eyes were wide with possibility, and Dr. Davis's measured nods provided a rhythm to our brainstorming session.

"Think about mentorship programs," I suggested, leaning back in my chair, letting my gaze drift to the celestial posters adorning my office walls. "We could connect professionals with these kids for hands-on learning experiences."

"Exactly!" Jamal leaned forward, the energy radiating off him making my webcam flicker. "They need role models who look like them, who've walked the same streets they do."

Dr. Davis, her demeanor as calm and collected as ever, added thoughtfully, "And perhaps we should consider summer science camps. Give them a place where curiosity is nurtured outside of school walls."

I rubbed my chin, the familiar texture of my beard under my fingertips—a grounding sensation amidst the flights of thought. It was this mix of tactile reality and expansive dreaming that always brought me back to center. "What about pairing up with local tech companies for summer internships?"

"Brilliant," Dr. Davis affirmed, her blue eyes catching the light from her screen. "Real-world experience could be invaluable."

"Can you imagine?" Jamal leaned closer to the camera, practically buzzing with energy. "Taking what they learn in class and actually applying it? That'd be dope!"

"Indeed," I said, a smile playing on my lips. The term 'dope' wasn't part of my usual vernacular, but its use by Jamal was infectious, bridging the gap between academia and the streets we were trying to uplift.

"Okay, let's consolidate these ideas and start reaching out," I continued. "The sooner we get this off the ground, the better."

"Count me in for anything you need, Langston," Dr. Davis offered, her voice firm yet supportive.

"Thanks, Simone," I replied, acknowledging not only her willingness to help but also the shared vision that connected us beyond our research and classrooms.

"Remember," she added, "this is just the beginning. You're building something that will resonate for generations."

Her words settled within me, a reminder of the dual legacy I hoped to leave: one written in the stars and another etched into the lives of those who dared to dream.

"Langston, I must say, your dedication to this cause is admirable," Dr. Davis said. "You're not only supporting Jamal's project but also nurturing the seeds of change in your old neighborhood. It's commendable."

"Thanks, Simone. It means a lot coming from you."

"Plus, with the recent grant you secured for your research," she continued, "it's clear you're on a trajectory that's as promising as any comet we've chased in our studies. You have a long and bright future ahead, Langston, and I dare say, you're becoming quite the face of our profession."

"Speaking of faces," Jamal interjected, his grin spreading wide enough to fill the screen, "Langston here has been dubbed the 'Sexy Scientist' on social media. Do we have the Sexy Scientist of the Year Award? If that doesn't get kids interested in astrophysics, I don't know what will!"

Laughter erupted from the group, a series of digital chuckles that bridged the distance between us. I couldn't help but laugh along, despite the feeling of embarrassment I was pushing down.

"Thank you, Jamal, for ensuring that title follows me into every professional setting," I said, my tone light but lined with playful sarcasm.

"Hey, it's all about making science appealing, right?" Jamal shot back, his eyes twinkling with mischief.

"Indeed, if it draws more attention to our field and inspires the next generation, then I'll bear the title proudly," I conceded, allowing myself to revel in the camaraderie and shared sense of purpose that filled the virtual room.

"Congratulations, Professor Wilkerson," one of the other professionals chimed in, their voice laced with humor. "May your newfound fame bring enlightenment to the masses."

"Let's just hope it brings them to the telescope rather than to my Instagram," I quipped, earning another round of laughter from the group.

This was exciting. We were creating — a bridge between two worlds I belonged to. And perhaps, through this initiative, I'd finally reconcile the man in the mirror with the stars he so loved to study.

"Alright, everyone, I think we've got a solid plan in place. Let's regroup next week with updates," I said, my gaze lingering on the screen a moment longer before ending the video conference. The faces of potential and promise disappeared, leaving only my reflection trapped in the monitor – grad student Langston from South Side staring back at tenured Professor Wilkerson.

"Ready to roll out?" Jamal asked, his voice cutting through the silence that had enveloped the office.

"Absolutely. Let's not keep the future astronomers waiting," I replied, standing up from my desk with a stretch. I reached for my jacket, which hung on the back of my chair, the fabric brushing against my fingers like a prelude to the night sky we were about to unveil to eager young minds.

We parted ways with Dr. Davis, who would join us later a the program's kickoff event. We descended the stairs of the university building, the echoes of our footfalls seemed to match the rhythm of anticipation drumming in my chest. Jamal was talking animatedly beside me, his enthusiasm infectious, but my thoughts were a step ahead, envisioning the community center buzzing with activity.

Before we could reach the car, my phone vibrated in my pocket, its insistent buzz pulling me back to the present. I glanced at the incoming call—Malcolm's name flashed across the screen—and a grin spread across my face.

"Langston! Man, you better hurry. This place is filling up fast, and it's not just the kids who are excited to see you. We've got local politicians, reporters... It's a full house!" Malcolm's voice was alive with excitement, painting a vibrant picture even before I could respond.

"Sounds like a star-studded event," I joked, playing off his energy as I slid into the driver's seat. "We're on our way. Just making sure we don't speed past any planets en route."

"Ha! Just don't take too long, or they might start thinking I'm the main attraction. You know I can't compete with the 'Sexy Scientist,' but a sexy-ass poetic social worker can do some damage," he quipped, and I could almost see his playful smirk through the phone.

"Trust me, your charm is unparalleled," I assured him, the familiar banter grounding me. "But give us thirty minutes. And Malcolm, thanks for being there."

"Always, brother. Oh, and your girl is here already--looking fire. Remember she recorded the accompanying vocals for my project? Aurora said she's planning to pitch the idea of including the spoken word poems in her upcoming project. Isn't that amazing?"

I was instantly excited. Two of my favorite people helping each other make dreams come true sounded amazing.

"That's great man!"

"I know. I didn't expect her to do that. I'm so excited. But we'll talk more later. See you soon." He ended the call.

"Seems like we might be walking into a bit of a frenzy," I said to Jamal, who was already buckling his seatbelt.

"Good thing you're an expert at navigating celestial storms, huh?" Jamal replied with a chuckle, and I couldn't help but laugh.

"Something like that," I mused as I started the engine. The hum of the car melded with the symphony of the city beyond.

As we sped through the city streets, my thoughts danced between the anticipation of the event and the thrill of Aurora's recent success. Everything seemed to fall into place: Aurora's blossoming career, Jamal's vision for the non-profit, and my own breakthroughs in astrophysics research. But above it all, the guiding star that shone brightest in my heart was Aurora. Her spirit, her resilience, and her unwavering passion were constant sources of inspiration.

"Life is funny, isn't it?" I mused aloud, my gaze drifting towards the horizon. "A few months ago, I couldn't have imagined any of this."

"True," Jamal agreed. "But sometimes, the universe has a way of surprising us. And you know what they say about stars, right?"

"Enlighten me," I urged, intrigued by his train of thought.

"Even in the darkest moments, they shine the brightest."

I rolled my eyes at his cheesy saying but smiled because recently life had proven him right. The journey thus far hadn't been easy, but it had brought me to a place where I could embrace my identity, my roots, and my love for Aurora.

As we pulled up to the community center, I could feel a sense of excitement in the air. The building was buzzing with activity. Ezekiel Reed, who'd owned the same local hardware store back when I was a kid, leaned on his cane as he spoke with the mayor. A bit over from the pair was City Councilwoman Denis Harper, who I'd once met at a speak engagement at a local high school. Laker's center Devon Rogers towered over the room, a smile on his face as he signed things for the fans that gathered around him.

The grand opening of the telescope room was packed.

But what touched my heart most were the local children who had come to witness the event, their eyes filled with wonder and curiosity. They looked up to me with the same awe usually reserved for Lakers players and Grammy rappers, and it was both humbling and inspiring.

"Look at them," I said to Jamal, gesturing towards the young crowd. "They remind me so much of us when we were kids, dreaming about the stars and the universe."

Jamal nodded, his expression thoughtful. "And now you're here, showing them that those dreams can become a reality. You're making a difference, Professor."

I had barely walked in before I was met by a group of people. I stood amidst the throng of eager faces, and with every handshake and smile exchanged serving I could see the community's pride in one of their own. Questions were hurled my way about the telescopes, the stars, and my journey.

I tried to glance around for Aurora. Having her next to me was the only thing missing at that moment.

"Dr. Wilkerson, how does it feel to be an inspiration to these young minds?" asked a local reporter, her recorder poised to catch my response.

"It's truly an honor," I began trying to keep my voice steady and sincere. "But let me redirect your attention to the real star here today—our future scientist Jamal."I placed a hand on the teenager's shoulder, drawing him closer into the limelight. "This initiative is a testament to the curiosity and potential of young people like him."

I wanted the attention to stay where it belonged: science and its ability to change lives.

Besides, I didn't want to do interviews. I didn't want to be famous. I just wanted my stars and Aurora.

And then, as if summoned by my silent yearning, the scent of her coconut hair oil hit me first – same aroma that lingered on my pillowcase since she'd started leaving her satin bonnet at my place last month. Aurora moved through the crowd with a grace that seemed to make the very air around her sing. Today, her beautiful curls cascaded in a wild, free-flowing halo that framed her expressive eyes and high cheekbones. She wore a simple yet elegant dress of deep burgundy, hugging her petite, curvy figure in all the right places and accentuating her caramel-colored skin. Her presence was a melody, a visual symphony that demanded attention without uttering a single note.

I couldn't help but smile as Aurora made her way to me, my eyes never leaving her enchanting figure. Inwardly, I marveled at how much my life had changed since meeting her. It was difficult growing up in the inner city. My interests didn't align with my environment. But now, as a black man who had risen above his circumstances, I was comfortable in my own skin and proud of the path I had chosen. All that was missing was a queen by my side.

"Langston!" she called out, weaving through the last few steps between us. She wrapped her arms around my neck and pulled me into a tender, loving kiss. The world seemed to fall away, leaving only the two of us in this perfect moment.

"Hey, lovebirds," Malcolm chimed in, nudging us apart with a wide grin on his face. "Aunt Cecily's on the other side of the room."

"Thanks, Malcolm," I replied, still a little breathless from our public display of affection. Since the confrontation with Marcus she'd been so happy to hold and kiss me in public with no shame. And damn if it didn't make me proud to have a woman like her on my arm.

With Aurora's hand firmly in mine, we made our way through the crowd. As we approached, we saw Aunt Cecily standing near Jamal. Between them stood a covered piece of art, its mysterious form only hinting at the beauty beneath. The media had gathered around, their cameras and microphones poised to capture the moment.

"Langston, Aurora," Aunt Cecily greeted us with a warm smile, the glint in her eyes revealing her excitement for what was about to be unveiled.

"Hey, Aunt Cecily! What's going on here?" Aurora asked..

"Jamal has something he'd like to share," she replied, nodding toward the young man beside her. Jamal looked both nervous and proud, his chest puffed out as he prepared to address the crowd.

"Good evening, everyone," Jamal began, his voice strong and steady. "I just wanted to take a moment to express my gratitude for being able to share my love of science with kids from my neighborhood." He paused, looking over at me. "I wouldn't be here today if it weren't for my mentor, Professor Langston Wilkerson. He's one of the first men who showed me that my dreams were attainable."

A surge of pride and emotion welled up inside me. To know that I had played such a significant role in Jamal's life and helped him find his passion was humbling. My own thoughts echoed his sentiment; I knew what it was like to struggle to find your place in the world. And I knew how important it was to find people who accepted you in your own skin without question.

"Thank you, Jamal," I said, my voice thick with emotion.

"Alright, let's not get too sappy now," Malcolm teased, lightening the mood. We all laughed and turned our attention back to the covered artwork, anticipation building as the moment of revelation drew near.

"Without further ado," Jamal continued, "I would like to introduce the renowned local sculptor, Ms. Cecily Raine. She has generously donated a piece of art to the community center, which will reside in our newly dedicated Astronomy room." The crowd clapped and Aunt Cecily smiled graciously.

"Thank you, Jamal," Aunt Cecily said, her voice strong and clear. "It is an honor to contribute to such an important cause." With a flourish, she pulled away the cover, revealing the stunning artwork beneath.

The piece was breathtaking. The sculpture stood tall in the center of the room, its metallic surface glistening under the soft glow of the gallery lights set up for its display. It consisted of a central core made of polished silver, resembling a celestial body at the heart of the universe. From this core radiated delicate tendrils of metal, each one representing a different star or constellation. They twisted and turned, intertwining in an elegant dance that mirrored the vastness and complexity of the cosmos. I hadn't realized how very talented Cecily was until this moment, because in the middle of her masterful metallic beauty was a raw-looking piece of molded clay that had been painted in earthy colors. All of the metal stars shot out from it.

It was the clay piece Aurora and I had made that day together in the studio weeks ago. Aunt Cecily had kept it, and put it right at the center of the piece.

Damn. She saved it like she knew this moment was coming. My heart swelled with appreciation for Aunt Cecily's thoughtfulness and talent. She had taken two separate worlds – the one Aurora and I had shared in creating our art, and the world of science we were celebrating today – and seamlessly blended them into one stunning masterpiece. The clay center seemed to pulse with energy, as if it remember that first pottery lesson where Aurora's thigh pressed against me under warm studio lights.

Aurora moved from my side, tears forming in her eyes. She'd recognized the piece too.

"The world is full of beautiful, amazing things. But at the center is us. Fragile. And we might even seem a bit weak.. But from us can come some amazing things."

"Auntie, this is beautiful." Aurora looked as if she were about to cry.

Her Aunt hugged her, then grabbed both our hands and smiled. "You two inspired it all. It's only right that this is where it ends up."

Jamal nudged me gently, bringing my attention back to the crowd that had gathered around us. Their eyes were expectant, waiting for me to speak. I took a deep breath and stepped forward, addressing everyone present.

"Thank you all for being here today," I began, my voice steady. "This dedication ceremony marks the beginning of an incredible journey – not just for our non-profit organization, but for the countless young minds who will walk through these doors and discover the beauty of the universe."

I glanced at Aurora, her eyes glistening with pride, and continued. "The stars above have inspired mankind for centuries, guiding adventurers, dreamers, and lovers alike. They serve as beacons of hope, reminding us that even in the darkest nights, there is always light to be found."

Aurora's hand slipped into mine, and I squeezed it gently, my words taking on a double meaning as I spoke of our own journey together. "And as we embark on this new adventure, I am confident that we will light the way for future generations to explore the cosmos and reach for the stars."

"None of this would have been possible without the support of our community, and especially the incredible talent of Aunt Cecily, whose beautiful artwork captures the essence of what we strive to achieve here." I gestured to the stunning sculpture, its metallic stars gleaming under the soft lighting of the room.

"Let this art piece be a reminder of the power of science and art, and how they can create something truly magical when combined," I concluded, my eyes never leaving Aurora's.

As the room erupted in applause, I couldn't help but feel an overwhelming sense of hope and optimism, both for the future of our non-profit and for the life Aurora and I were building together. We had weathered the storm, emerging stronger and more resilient than ever before.

I slipped my arm around her, softly kissing her on the lips. As our lips parted, her bitten-lower-lip smirk told me tonight we wouldn't be studying constellations – we'd chart new ones beneath sweat-damp sheets.

Epilogue

Aurora

In the sun-drenched studio, my fingers glided over the strings of the bass guitar, each note humming with newfound freedom. It had been a year—a year of metamorphosis, of shedding the weight of the past and embracing the buoyancy of the present. My first solo album was more than just a collection of songs; it was an odyssey of my soul, each track a footprint on the journey to self-discovery.

"Take five, Aurora," Maria called out, her voice warm with encouragement. Our partnership in this musical endeavor was a symbiotic one, built on mutual respect and artistic vision. To be understood, to be given creative control—it's what I had always yearned for, and now, it was reality.

After giving Maria a thumbs up and big smile, I set down my guitar and strolled over to the window to peer out at the Chicago skyline. The city was my canvas, its energy seeping into my music, giving it life.

I had made so many new connections to inspire my music, but Malcolm transformed my sound more than anyone else. I had asked his permission to include his spoken word poems as interludes throughout my album, and it .surpassed our wildest creative hopes. I could hear Malcolm's rich timbre reciting the poem that helped inspire the song we were working on today. His words were a gift, and added another layer of depth to my artistry. And I was already making notes and and jotting lyrics in my notebook for the next project.

Inspiration was a constant companion these days, nudging me at every turn, whispering lyrics into my ear as I lay awake at night, often cuddled up with Langston. New songs fluttered inside me like butterflies, eager to take flight. And when they did, they soared, unfettered and resplendent.

One of the biggest blessing was being able to run some of my rough lyrics past Aunt Cecily. She was a huge supporter. Conversations over tea were grounding, and being able to spend time with her was so important to me.

Maria came and stood next to me and showed me a video on her phone. It was a clip of me opening for a large artist that had been in town recently, and it had gone amazing. The notoriety Marcus had tried to give me had been turned into a blessing. A big smile spread across my face.

And as for Marcus himself? He was a distant memory, a shadow that no longer loomed over me. He had tried to reach out to me after those viral videos had his facade like sugar in boiling water - dissolving until nothing remained but bitter residue. It was the same crap about how we were meant to be together and how we complimented each other. He didn't get there was no more *we* until the Chicago Tribune headlines declared MY victory over his gaslight symphony. It was the final nail in the coffin of his career, and I had hammered it in. Three voicemails lingered unplayed - his voice probably carried the tinny desperation of strangers who mistake exits for invitations that his previous ones did. Money and clout had slipped through his fingers like sand, and with them, his hold on me.

"You headed home?" Maria asked as she walked to get her jacket. It had been a good session, but I was definitely ready to call it for the day. I stretched and smiled at her comfortable use of the word "home" in reference to where I lived now.

I had moved to Chicago to live with Langston, and it was the best decision. Waking up to chat with him before he headed to the college, or spending evenings watching movies and eating Chinese, were just a few simple pleasures I didn't know I'd enjoy so much. And our love only grew stronger. I was so proud of his recent accomplishments in both his research and non-profit work.

Seeing him doodling math equations on a whiteboard I'd completely ignored previously was oddly satisfying. I mean watching the muscles flex through his faded tank top as he stood barefoot mulling over some math I couldn't possibly begin to understand, even though he'd tried to explain it, was fun. It was like watching him make his own music.

But what I loved most was seeing the look on his face whenever he worked with the non-profit he and Jamal ran.

I was so proud.

All I wanted to do after a long day at the studio was get home and wrap my arms around him. As if reading my mind, as soon as I arrived home Langston wrapped me in a warm embrace. Our lips met in a passionate kiss that ignited the fire within us both.

"I missed you," he mumbled into my ear, the hairs on his chin tickling my neck. He still sent shivers up my spine.

"I always miss you," I replied, letting my bag hit the ground, quickly followed by every piece of clothes both of us had on.

We made love tenderly this time. He still kept me guessing - slow hands one night, quick whispers of need the following night, with a demanding urgency the next. All our love making was amazing. And I was willing to give him all of me because he made me happier than I ever dreamed possible.

Langston

I was stretched out on the bed, one hand behind my back, staring at the ceiling. Aurora lay across my chest, her warm bare breast pressed to me, sound asleep. I wanted to wake up like this every morning.

My nomination letter for a prestigious award laid on the bedside table. It meant a flight to Europe for the ceremony. I saw Aurora's excitement when I told her last night. She seemed more excited to be on my arm supporting me than I was to actually be nominated. It made me smile.

The nomination right on the heels of receiving not just a renewal, but more money, for my research grant, meant times were good professionally.

But the best "award" that I had received was hung up next to the whiteboard in the other room. It was a handmade 'sirtificate' spelled out by the 6-year-old boy from the community center. He said it was because I was his favorite scientist after I showed him how to use the telescope at a special nighttime event Jamal had arranged.

Watching the joy in that kid's eyes--eyes mirroring mine at his age--that was the best award I could ask for.

I breathed in as I thought of the peace I had by embracing all of who I am – a black boy from a rough neighborhood that grew up to love the stars in the sky, a professor, a mentor, a friend, and a loving partner to Aurora.

Thinking of friends reminded me that I needed to drop by the studio to see Malcolm today. He was recording another poem for Aurora's album. Seeing one of my best friends living his dream thanks to a door opened by the woman of my dreams was amazing.

Aurora stirred on me a little. I turned my ear when I realized she was singing quietly in her sleep. I smirked realizing she was probably making new music at that moment and didn't even realize it. She'd been making so many new songs, and they were damn good. Some-times she'd perform them for me in private after a long day at work. Her music thrived while Marcus' career had crashed and burned.

I couldn't help but feel vindicated. I actually had to call Craig off Marcus, because my boy was going in. A few months ago during our standing DnD game I told Craig he didn't need to bother that broken loser anymore.

"Ah man, that was my hobby," was all Craig had said with a lopsided grin.

"It's cool," I said right before I rolled my dice to a number high enough to give the monster of Malcolm, the selected dungeon master, a death blow. As Malcolm cussed and complained, Craig and I kept talking.

"That Marcus dude was messing with a good woman. Man, I wish I could find one," Craig mused.

"She's out there. For both of y'all," I said, including Malcolm. "You'll find her one day. I for damn sure wasn't looking for Aurora the day she stepped into my life."

"Nah." Malcolm threw up his hands as if to ward off true love itself. "I'm cool as a player poet. I don't want no ball and chain."

Craig sucked his teeth and rolled. Another deathblow for Malcolm's other monster. "Well I want one," Craig said. "You sure Aurora don't have a sister? I heard her auntie fine, too."

I looked at Malcolm who shrugged.

"No man," I said. "You gonna have to find someone not related to mine. I ain't trying to see you at the family reunion."

Thinking back to the cussing out I got from him made me laugh. My movement made Aurora stir again, and the press of her body against mine derailed my train of thought. I wasn't planning on it, but I just might have to wake her up.

Aurora yawned and stretched, her body arching into mine. "You're thinking out loud again," she mumbled. "What's on your mind?"

Even through the silk scarf she wore I could smell her shampoo. "You. Us. Our future."

She tilted her head up, eyes blinking open. A slow, sultry smile spread across her face. "Yeah? You got plans for me, Professor Wilkerson?"

"Maybe a few," I said, tracing a finger down her arm. "How do you feel about another Chicago winter?"

Aurora's brows furrowed. "Cold. Why?"

I took a deep breath and reached for the drawer of my nightstand, fingers closing around a small velvet box. I'd had a special piece commissioned where the larger engagement stone reminded me of the colors in the Eagle Nebula, and the wedding band I'd add later had two smaller ones designed to flush up on both sides in a nod to what she called her 'lucky constellation,' Orion's belt.

"Because I was thinking maybe we should get away a bit, somewhere warm. Just the two of us. But before we plan trips... there's something I need to ask you."

Also by Morgan Sterling

Nerdy Affair Series

Stellar Harmony:https://books2read.com/stellarharmony/
Soft Reset: https://dl.bookfunnel.com/dnecwccwgt
Binary Bonds: Coming Soon

Braided Realm Series

Golden Melodies: https://books2read.com/u/47BKzA
Embers of Harmony: Coming Soon

Let's Keep In Touch

Follow me for updates, behind-the-scenes content, and more:

- **Instagram**: https://www.instagram.com/author.morgan.sterling/

- **Facebook**: https://www.facebook.com/authormorgansterling

- **Blue Sky**: https://bsky.app/profile/authormsterling.bsky.social

- **Threads**: https://www.threads.net/@author.morgan.sterling

- **Tik Tok**: https://www.tiktok.com/@author.morgan.ste

- **X**: https://x.com/AuthorMSterling

- **Website**: https://authormorgansterling.com

Feel free to email me at author.morgan.sterling@gmail.com with your thoughts or questions—I'd love to hear from you!

About the author

Morgan Sterling writes captivating romance and romantasy stories that celebrate the beauty of self-discovery, nerdy connections, and heartfelt love. When she's not weaving tales, you can find her exploring sci-fi worlds, reading a comic under a cozy blanket, or spending time with her family. Her other hobbies include building and wearing cosplays and 3D printing. Connect with Morgan at https://author morgansterling.com

Soft Reset preview

Chapter 1

Jamal

The telescope's powerful lens shimmered in the dim light, beckoning the eager crowd closer. Standing before them, I felt the weight of their eyes—and the stars above. I absentmindedly ran my fingers over the intricate details of the 3D-printed solar system model in my pocket. It was a comforting, grounding weight that calmed my nerves.

"Welcome, stargazers!" I heard my voice carried across the makeshift amphitheater. "Tonight, we're not only looking up; we're journeying through the cosmos."

A soft whirl of telescopes being adjusted punctuated the silence that followed. The rich aroma of hot chocolate wafted from a nearby stand, blending with the earthy tang of fresh grass and the occasional spark of jasmine on the breeze. In the distance, crickets provided a soothing natural soundtrack. It was calming.

"Now, who can tell me which constellation looks like a giant cosmic spoon?" I asked, grinning as several hands shot up. I called on a boy who looked to be about eight. "That's right, the Big Dipper! Though personally, I always thought it looked more like a celestial ladle. Maybe the universe loves soup?"

Laughter rippled through the crowd, and I let out a long breath. Things were going well. I'd practiced this presentation countless times in my basement apartment, but the energy of the live audience was intoxicating.

As the laughter subsided, I pointed towards another cluster of stars. "Now, let's take a journey to the constellation Orion. Can anyone spot the three stars that make up Orion's belt?"

A chorus of "ooh"s and "ahh"s filled the air as people craned their necks, searching the night sky. I couldn't help but smile, remembering my own wonderstruck moments as a kid.

"You know, when I was younger, my grandma used to tell me those three stars were actually a celestial BBQ grill." I chuckled, earning more laughs from the crowd. "She'd say, 'Jamal, even the gods need a good cookout now and then.' And let me tell you, the idea of cosmic ribs was pretty appealing to a hungry kid."

I paused, letting the image sink in. "But here's the cool part - while my grandma's story was only for fun, the stars in Orion's belt are cooking up something incredible. They're nurseries for new stars, forging the building blocks of entire solar systems in their cosmic furnaces."

A collective gasp rippled through the audience. I could see the wonder in their eyes, mirroring the twinkling stars above.

As I guided the community through the night sky, pointing out constellations and sharing tidbits of astronomical trivia, I couldn't help but marvel at how far I'd come. A few years ago, I was that shy kid in the back of the classroom, dreaming of the stars but too afraid to speak up.

Now, here I was, leading a community stargazing event, the founder of STEM Roots Foundation. It was an odd feeling—a mix of pride and pressure. I scanned the faces for Langston, my mentor who was somewhere in the crowd.

"And there," I said, gesturing towards a bright point in the sky, "is Jupiter. Fun fact: if Earth were the size of a grape, Jupiter would be the size of a basketball. Though I wouldn't recommend trying to dunk it."

More chuckles from the audience. I felt my dimple deepen as I smiled, letting my honey-brown eyes scan the crowd again. My eyes roved for a moment, then cut back to a face at the back of the crowd. Sierra? My heart skipped a beat, but I swiftly refocused on the task at hand.

"Now, who's ready to take a closer look through our telescopes?"

As the crowd eagerly moved towards the instruments I looked around again, but that face was gone. So I guided an excited child towards one of the telescopes, and let my mind drift.

High school me would've been hiding in the library right now. Instead, I was here—hosting a stargazing event and leading my own nonprofit. Wild.

I glanced around, hoping to catch another glimpse of Sierra—if it was indeed her I'd seen earlier. Part of me longed for her to witness how far I'd come, to see me as more than the "brainy kid" she'd known in school.

"Hey, little astronaut," I kneeled beside the child at the telescope. "What do you see up there?"

As the kid excitedly described the craters on the moon, I had to smile. This was why I'd started STEM Roots—to ignite that same passion in others that had driven me. But with that warmth came a familiar twinge of doubt.

I am technically still a teen. Nine*teen*. An extraordinary nineteen-year-old, soon-to-be twenty-year-old. One that is used to sitting in the room with much older people discussing the origins of the universe.

And my body was that of a man. I was prepubescent in high school, having skipped so many years. But now when my lean, athletic frame unfolded to its full height I was usually a head or two taller than most people. At nineteen, I had already grown into a man's body, with broad shoulders and defined muscles visible even beneath my fitted NASA t-shirt. I kept my short, curly hair neatly trimmed. I had learned that if they were going to look at me because I was a young black male in a space where almost no one ever looked like me, I had to look like I had my shit together all the time.

But the truth was that inside me the small boy I used to be was still there. The one who tried to hide in the corners even though he knew some teacher was about to make all the kids look at him for the answer. And I hated it, because I knew one day everyone would look at me, and I wouldn't have the answer.

My internal wrestling match was interrupted by a familiar, deep voice.

"Quite the turnout you've got here, Jamal."

I turned to see Langston, my mentor's eyes twinkling with pride. The sight of him—successful, respected, and still deeply connected to the community—both inspired and intimidated me. Tonight he was mostly staying toward the edge of the crowd, though occasionally a kid would scamper over to show him something, or a woman would try her luck by pretending to have some silly question. He took it all in grace. He was used to the unsought attention. After all, there weren't too many young black astrophysics professors that looked like they belonged on a BET movie.

"Dr. Wilkerson," I greeted him, straightening up. "I'm glad you could make it. What do you think of the event so far?"

Langston's warm smile widened as he extended his hand.

"You've got the crowd hooked, Jamal," Langston said, his voice low and measured. "Now, let's work on making them fall in love with the stars too."

"Thanks, Dr. Wilkerson. I'm trying to strike a balance between the science and keeping it accessible."

Langston nodded, his expression thoughtful. "That's the key. Remember, these folks aren't only here for facts. They're here for wonder. Show them the poetry in the cosmos."

My mind raced with ideas. "Like connecting the constellations to local stories?"

"Exactly," Langston replied, his eyes lighting up. "Make the stars feel like they belong to them."

Langston rested a hand on my shoulder. "You're doing more than hosting a stargazing event, Jamal. You're inspiring them. Don't lose sight of why you started this."

As we discussed strategies, I realized how odd it was. Langston grew up in this neighborhood decades before me. And he left it, but came back to build it up. I was fortunate to have found him.

Our conversation was interrupted by a booming voice. "Yo, Professor Stardust! You gonna hog all the telescopes or what?"

I turned to see Terrance striding towards us, his infectious grin already spreading across his face. Despite the teasing, a wave of relief washed over me at my best friend's arrival.

"Terrance," I laughed, dapping him up. "I thought you said you had to work."

"Yeah, well," Terrance shrugged, his eyes twinkling with mischief, "someone's gotta make sure you don't float off into space, right?"

I stood flanked by two people who were so supportive. Between Langston's wisdom and Terrance's humor, I felt calmer.

This wasn't the first Stargazing event the non-profit had organized—but it was the first one that Langston had stepped back and let me run solo.

Terrance's gaze swept over the gathered crowd, his eyebrows rising in appreciation. "Man, you've got half the neighborhood out here. Not bad for a bunch of floating rocks, huh?"

I chuckled, shaking my head. "They're not just rocks, T. They're—"

"Whole worlds waiting to be explored," Terrance finished, mimicking my tone. "Yeah, yeah, I've heard your TED talk, remember?"

Langston laughed, but before I could retort, a small boy tugged at his sleeve, eyes wide with curiosity. "Mister, can I see the stars?"

Langston's face softened. "Sure thing, little man. Let's go check out Saturn while Jamal here preps for his next lecture."

As Langston guided the child to a nearby telescope, I watched Terrance make his way to a small group gathered at another on. I felt a swell of gratitude. Terrance's easy manner bridged the gap between my scientific enthusiasm and the community's more relaxed vibe. He'd been doing that since we were kids—building a bridge between me, the oddball, and our community.

My thoughts were interrupted by a familiar laugh cutting through the night air. My heart skipped a beat as I scanned the crowd, searching for its source.

There, at the edge of the gathering, stood Sierra Daniels. I was right earlier when I thought I'd glimpsed her—my high school crush. I'd been out of the neighborhood mostly since I graduated high school years ago—only coming home to sleep, hang out with Terrance and maybe shoot some hoops. I essentially spend all my waking hours on campus. Whatever Sierra had been up to had kept her on a different path. This was the first time I'd seen her in a long time, and damn it if little Jamal didn't feel for a moment like crawling away somewhere to hide.

I swallowed hard, my fingers unconsciously fidgeting with the tiny 3D-printed solar system in my pocket. Sierra's presence was unexpected, she hadn't been to any of the organization's previous events. I watched as she moved through the crowd, her fitted blazer and graphic tee showing she still had great taste.

"You gonna stare all night, or you gonna talk to her?" Terrance's voice startled me.

"I wasn't... I mean, I didn't..." I stammered, feeling heat rise to my cheeks.

Terrance chuckled, clapping a hand on my shoulder. "Man, you haven't changed since high school. Go on, Professor Galaxy. Show her your stars."

I took a deep breath, steeling myself. "Right. It's just Sierra. No big deal."

As I made my way towards her, Sierra turned, her eyes widening in recognition. "Jamal? Is that you?"

"Hey, Sierra," I managed, my voice steadier than I felt. "Glad you could make it to our stargazing night."

Sierra's smile was warm, but I noticed a flicker of something—surprise? uncertainty?—in her eyes. "Wouldn't miss it. My boss comes to these, and she told me I should check it out. This is incredible, what you're doing here."

I felt a surge of pride, momentarily forgetting my nerves. "Thanks. It's all about bringing science to the community, you know? Making it accessible."

"I can see that," Sierra nodded, her gaze drifting to the sea of eager faces around us. "You've really found your calling, huh?"

As we talked I couldn't help but wonder what Sierra had been up to all this time. I wanted to ask, but something held me back. She was talking, but she seemed shielded somehow. Instead of pushing her, I gestured towards a nearby telescope. "Want to take a look? Saturn's particularly clear tonight."

As Sierra leaned closer, her hair brushing my arm, my pulse quickened. Seeing her wonder reminded me why I loved the stars—they made everything feel possible. I inhaled sharply, catching a whiff of her familiar scent—cocoa butter and something floral.

She hadn't changed a bit.

"Sure, I'd love to," Sierra said, her voice softer now that we were standing closer.

As she leaned in to peer through the eyepiece, I studied her profile. The years had only enhanced her beauty, adding a maturity to her features that made my breath catch. When she looked back at me I averted my gaze, focusing on adjusting the telescope.

"Oh wow," Sierra breathed. "I can see the rings!"

I grinned, unable to contain my enthusiasm. "Pretty amazing, right? Did you know that Saturn's rings are made up of billions of particles of ice and rock?"

Sierra straightened up, her eyes sparkling with interest. "Really? Tell me more."

For a moment, I forgot who I was talking to and launched into an explanation about the composition of Saturn's rings. As I spoke, I noticed Sierra watching intently, a small smile playing on her lips.

"What?" I asked self-consciously.

"Nothing," she shook her head, that dimple in her right cheek making an appearance. "It's... you've changed, Jamal. But in a good way."

Before I could respond, I felt a nudge from behind. Terrance had sidled up next to me, a mischievous grin on his face.

"Hate to interrupt the astronomy lesson, but we've got some kids over here dying to see Jupiter," Terrance said, his eyes darting between us. "I don't know how to line up this fancy telescope, man."

I hesitated, torn between my responsibilities and my desire to keep talking to Sierra. I opened my mouth to speak, but Sierra beat me to it.

"Go on," she said, her smile understanding. "Your fans are waiting, Professor Galaxy."

As I walked away, my mind raced with questions and possibilities. I glanced back over my shoulder, catching Sierra's eye one last time before she melted into the crowd.

I spent the next hour guiding the last few stargazers through their celestial observations. The spring night air had cooled, carrying the faint scent of jasmine from a nearby garden. As I powered down the final telescope, my eyes swept across the dwindling crowd, searching for Sierra.

There she was, leaning against a tree, her silhouette illuminated by the soft glow of a nearby streetlamp. My fingers instinctively reached for the miniature solar system model in my pocket, my thumb tracing the ridges of Saturn's rings.

Should I go over there? What if she's only being polite? But then again, she stayed till the end...

"You stuck in neutral again?" Terrance's voice cut through my thoughts.

I shook my head. "I'm going, I'm going."

I made my way towards Sierra, each step feeling both terrifying and exhilarating.

"Hey. Glad you could make it tonight."

Sierra's smile was warm, genuine. "Me too. It's been a while, hasn't it?"

"Yeah, since high school," I nodded, leaning against the tree next to her. "So, what'd you think of the show? Not too nerdy, I hope?"

Sierra laughed, the sound sending a shiver down my spine. "Are you kidding? It was fascinating. I had no idea you were so... passionate about all this."

"I guess I didn't show that side of myself much back then. I mean I was a kid, I didn't hangout with you guys in school."

"Well, I'm glad I got to see it now," Sierra said.

My heart quickened. I fought the urge to fidget with the solar system model, instead gesturing towards the telescopes. "You know, I've been running these events for a while now. Part of the STEM Roots Foundation I started last year."

Sierra's eyebrows raised, a flicker of surprise crossing her face. "You started the foundation? Wow, Jamal. That's... impressive."

I shrugged, aiming for nonchalance but feeling a swell of pride. "Trying to give back, you know? Share the wonders of science with the community."

"Always the brainiac," Sierra teased, but her tone was warm. "Some things never change."

I grinned and leaned in a bit. "Oh, I don't know about that. I'd like to think I've evolved a bit since high school. Maybe even picked up a few smooth moves along the way."

Sierra's laugh was interrupted by an elderly woman approaching us, her eyes bright with excitement.

"Young man," she said, grasping my hand. "I wanted to thank you for this wonderful evening. My grandson was absolutely captivated."

"I'm so glad to hear that, Mrs. Johnson. Will we see Kevin at the coding workshop next week?"

As I chatted with Mrs. Johnson, I caught Sierra watching me from the corner of my eye. Her expression had shifted, a mix of curiosity and... was that admiration? The realization was a bit thrilling, making me stand a little straighter.

More community members approached, each offering thanks and praise. I responded to each with genuine warmth, but my awareness of Sierra's presence never faded.

As the last well-wisher drifted away, I turned back to Sierra, heart racing. The night air had cooled, and I could see her breath misting in the soft glow of the streetlights.

"So," I began, searching for a way to recapture the earlier ease, "remember that time in Mr. Grayson's physics class when I accidentally set off the fire alarm during our rocket experiment?"

Sierra's eyes lit up with laughter. "You mean *your* rocket experiment. Our assignment was to make a paper airplane that flew 10 feet. You were so extra. How could I forget? You looked like you were about to faint when the principal showed up."

I chuckled, running a hand through my short curls. "Not my finest moment. But hey, at least it got us out of that pop quiz."

Our shared laughter faded into a comfortable silence. I studied Sierra's face, noting the subtle changes since high school. There was a new confidence in her posture, a determination in her eyes that hadn't been there before.

"What about you?" I asked, genuinely curious. "How's it going?"

Sierra's smile faltered. "It's... a work in progress," she said, her fingers fidgeting with the strap of her purse. "I work at Ms. Rosa's. I took some computer classes at the library for coding and building apps and stuff. It's hard though."

I nodded, sensing her hesitation. "I can imagine. Got any ideas in the works?" When she nodded I prompted, "What's the concept?"

"It's meant to connect local businesses and artist in need of space with local brick-and-mortars in need of cash," Sierra explained, her voice growing more animated. "Like, if a local painter wanted to do a showcase of their work but couldn't afford to rent a gallery, they could probably give Ms. Witcome who runs that soup kitchen some money. I mean clear the spot out after they serve dinner and it's huge. And I know the kitchen could use the money."

Sierra shrugged as if her idea wasn't great.

"That's brilliant!" My mind was already racing with possibilities. "Have you considered..."

I caught myself, not wanting to overwhelm her with suggestions. Instead, I switched gears, "What's been the biggest challenge so far?"

Sierra sighed, her shoulders slumping. "Honestly? Everything. Coding, funding, just... believing it's possible, I guess."

I felt a surge of empathy—I knew that feeling all too well. "I get that. When I first started STEM Roots, there were days I thought I was in way over my head."

Sierra's eyes widened with surprise. "Seriously? But you seem so... together."

I chuckled, absent-mindedly fidgeting with the small 3D-printed solar system model in my pocket. "Trust me, it's all smoke and mirrors. But you know what helped? Having people around who believed in me, even when I didn't."

I paused, considering my next words carefully. "Hey, we've got some coding workshops coming up at STEM Roots. Nothing fancy, just a chance for folks to learn and share ideas. You should come."

Sierra hesitated, her fingers twisting a coil of her hair. "I don't know... I'm not exactly a coding prodigy."

"Neither am I," I admitted with a grin. "But that's the beauty of it. We're all learning together." I let my voice take on a playful tone. "Plus, I could use someone to keep me on my toes. Can't let these kids think I know everything, right?"

Sierra laughed, a warm sound that made my heart thump. "Well, when you put it like that... maybe I could stop by."

"Great! I mean, cool. It'll be fun." I pulled out my phone, trying to appear casual. "Here, let me get your number. I can send you the details."

As Sierra recited her number, I couldn't help but think how different this felt from high school days. Back then, I would have stumbled over my words, too nervous to even look her in the eye. Now, there was an ease between us, a spark of something new and exciting.

"There," I said, saving her contact. "I'll text you the info later."

Sierra nodded, a small smile playing on her lips. "Thanks, Jamal."

As she turned to leave, I called out, "Hey, Sierra?" She looked back, eyebrow raised. "Your app idea? It's going to change lives. I can feel it."

As Sierra disappeared into the night, the warmth of her smile lingered like starlight. For the first time in years, I felt a pull—not only to the cosmos, but to something, someone, closer to home.

***

Soft Reset is a <u>free novella</u> that bridges books 1 and 2 in The Nerdy Affair series.
You get a copy right now by visiting
https://dl.bookfunnel.com/dnecwccwgt

Feedback?

If you enjoyed this story, **I'd love to hear from you!** Share your thoughts by emailing me <u>author.morgan.sterling@gmail.com</u> or tagging me on social media @authormorgansterling. Your feedback not only brightens my day but helps me grow as a storyteller. Thank you for your support!